Introduction

If you have read seasons #1 and #2 (books #1 to #24) of the Witch P.I. Mystery series, you can skip this section.

For those of you joining late, I would highly recommend you start at book one (Witch is When it all Began) in order to get the most enjoyment from the series. However, if you prefer to start with this book, what follows is a very brief rundown of what's happened so far.

Private investigator, Jill Gooder, is the star of the Witch P.I. Mysteries. Our story began when she discovered she was a witch. Since then, she's divided her life between the human world (in Washbridge), the supernatural world (in Candlefield) and the ghost world (Ghost Town better known as GT). Jill is able to move between these three worlds at will. She has adventures in all three worlds.

Jill's birth family are spread over both Candlefield and Ghost Town. Grandma, Aunt Lucy, and Jill's cousins, twins: Amber and Pearl, live in Candlefield. Jill's mother, father and their new partners all live in GT.

In the human world, Jill's adoptive parents died some time ago, but she's still very close to her sister, Kathy, and Kathy's family: husband, Peter, and their two children, Lizzie and Mikey.

Jill's relationship with detective Jack Maxwell was rather fiery at first, but over time they fell in love and have now lived together for just over a year. When we last saw Jill (in the last book of season #2 - Witch is When It

Was Over), Jack had just asked her to marry him. Although there was nothing Jill wanted more than to say yes, she felt she must first share her secret with him. She told him she was a witch.

This book, the first one of season #3, picks up the story twelve months later.

Arguably, the star of these books is still Winky — a one-eyed cat who is completely crazy, as you'll soon find out.

I hope you enjoy the Witch P.I. Mysteries.

Adele Abbott.

Chapter 1

(Author's note: This is the first book of season three. It picks up the story twelve months after the previous book.)

When I arrived at my offices, I thought for a moment that I was in the wrong room. The furniture hadn't changed, but Mrs V's desk, the filing cabinets, and all the chairs were in the wrong place. Normally, Mrs V's desk was to my left, but this morning, it was to my right—over by the window. The filing cabinets, which were usually at the far side of the office, were to my left where Mrs V's desk would normally be.

"Morning, Jill." Mrs V was looking exceptionally pleased with herself. "What do you think of the new look?"

"I—err—did *you* move all the furniture around?"

"With my old bones?" She laughed. "It takes me all my time to get up the stairs these days. Brian and his assistant did it yesterday."

"And Brian is?"

"Brian Briggs. He's a grandmaster."

"A chess player?"

"No, dear. Not that kind of grandmaster. He's a Feng Shui grandmaster."

"*Feng Shui*? Isn't that just nonsense?"

"Certainly not." She tutted. "Feng Shui was developed by the Chinese; it helps to harmonize people with their surrounding environment. That's what Brian says, and he should know. After all, he is a—"

"Grandmaster. Yes, so you said. Brian Briggs? He doesn't sound very Chinese."

"He isn't; he comes from Deptford, but he's studied Feng Shui for almost twenty years."

"How exactly did you come across him?"

"Do you remember Doreen Daggers?"

"Mrs D? Your synchronised knitting partner?"

"That's right. She'd been having so many problems with her dining room that she was almost on the point of despair."

"What kind of problems?"

"I didn't like to ask. Anyway, one of her friends put her in touch with Brian, and after he'd worked his Feng Shui magic, all her dining room problems disappeared. So, I got to thinking that this office has never felt quite right."

"How do you mean?"

"I've never been able to reach the same knitting speed here as I do at home."

"What about your actual work? You know, the stuff you do for me?"

"I don't have a problem with that because it only ever takes me a few minutes each day. It's the knitting that's the issue. At least, it was until Brian worked his magic." She held up her knitting—an orange and red scarf. "Look how much I've managed to get done already this morning. Twice what I would normally do."

"That's great. I do see one minor problem with this new layout, though."

"What's that, dear?"

"The socket for the landline is over the other side of the room where your desk used to be."

"Don't worry. I brought an extension lead from home."

"You mean this tripwire across the room? I'm not sure the clients will be impressed if they have to limbo underneath it."

"You're right. I'll give the phone company a call and get them to move the socket over to this side of the office. I don't imagine it will cost too much."

"Okay."

"By the way, Jill, Jules called me on Saturday."

"How's she doing?"

"She sounded very chipper. She's still with that nice young man, Dexter."

"They must have been together for over a year now."

"They have, and they're going to get engaged soon—she said we can both expect an invitation to the party."

"Great."

"It sounds like she's enjoying her new job too. The money's good, but she misses being able to knit because now she actually has some real work to do."

Ouch.

Jules had landed herself an admin role at Washbridge police station. I'd been sorry to see her go, but it was nice to get back to having just a single PA/receptionist. Two had been something of an overkill.

"I suppose I'd better make a start." I stepped over the tripwire. "Make sure you warn any visitors about this, won't you?"

"Of course. How are the wedding preparations going? You hardly ever talk about it."

"Jack's got everything in hand. Well, him and *Marceau*."

"The wedding planner?"

"Yeah. That man drives me to distraction. I thought his brother was bad, but Marceau is even worse. He's coming over again tonight."

Marceau Montage, our wedding planner, was the

brother of Maurice Montage, the interior designer/ballroom dancing instructor. Kathy had first come up with the idea of hiring a wedding planner, and suggested Marceau. I'd balked at the idea—how difficult could it be to organise a wedding? But Jack had thought it was a great idea and had somehow managed to persuade me we should do it. Since then, Jack seemed to spend more time with Marceau than he did with me.

"Have you had the final fitting for your dress, Jill?"

"Not yet. It's one night this week—Wednesday, I think."

"I can't wait to see it. I bet it's gorgeous."

"It ought to be. I could have bought a small holiday home for what it cost."

"Don't exaggerate. It'll all be worth it on the day."

"I guess so."

I'd done my best to persuade Jack that he and I should elope to Gretna Green, and get married in front of a couple of witnesses picked off the street, but he wouldn't hear of it. Don't get me wrong, I love Jack to bits, and wanted nothing more than to marry him and spend the rest of our lives together. But the wedding itself? Blah!

"Oh, I almost forgot, Jill. Your grandmother phoned just before you arrived. She wants you to go and see her."

Great! Just the start to a new week I'd been hoping for.

"Did she say where she was?"

"No. Sorry, I never thought to ask."

"No problem. I'll track her down later."

"She did say it was urgent."

"It always is where she's concerned."

When I went through to my office, Winky was on my

desk.

"What's that nutjob up to now?" he said.

"I assume you're referring to Mrs V?"

"Who else? The old bag lady was in here yesterday. She had some weird guy with her. How am I supposed to enjoy a quiet Sunday when they're moving furniture around? No consideration, some people."

"It's Feng Shui."

"Feng whatty?"

"Shui. The ancient Chinese art of talking cobblers."

"I don't know why you stand for it. This is your business, isn't it? You should give her the bullet and get Jules back here. I miss her pretty face."

"Jules is happy in her new job."

"How can she be, without me for company?"

"You're probably one of the reasons she left. And how many times do I have to tell you not to sit on my desk? Get down."

"You should be nice to me. I'm feeling quite fragile at the moment."

"*Fragile*? You? Do me a favour."

"It's true. I've taken some hard knocks recently."

"Such as?"

"First, my main money-spinner, the Midnight Gym, gets closed down. That's had a big impact on my finances."

"You should count yourself lucky you got away with that scam for as long as you did."

I-Sweat's membership had grown so quickly that they'd been forced to relocate to brand new, custom-built premises on the other side of town.

"Who's taking over their old place?"

"I've no idea. I haven't seen the landlord to ask him. It looks as though it's almost ready to open, though. The sign went up last week: Escape."

"What's that when it's at home?"

"No idea. Maybe a travel agent? *Escape* on holiday?"

"How am I supposed to make money out of that?"

"You're not."

"And then there's the disappointment over your wedding." He sighed.

"You're not still going on about that, are you?"

"Why wouldn't I? When the old bag lady got married, you promised that when you got hitched I could be your pagecat."

"I'm not sure I actually made a promise."

"Yes, you did, and now you've gone back on your word."

"My nephew, Mikey, is going to be my pageboy."

"He won't be as good at it as I would."

"That's as maybe, but it's too late to do anything about it now. The wedding is a week on Saturday."

"I feel so betrayed."

"Look, if Mikey is ill, you can stand in for him. I can't say fairer than that, can I?"

It was hard to believe that in less than two weeks Jack and I would be married. It was just over a year since Jack had proposed, and I'd shared my secret with him. On that day, I'd had no idea how he would react—I just knew that I couldn't continue to live a lie. If he'd been horrified by my revelation, I would have used magic to make him forget what he'd just seen and heard, and then walked away forever. To my surprise and delight, he'd been very accepting, although it's true to say he'd been in a state of shock for some considerable time. Once he'd recovered, we'd had many long discussions — one of the most important concerned how best to keep *our* secret. If word got out that Jack knew I was a witch, the rogue retrievers would take me to Candlefield where I'd be forced to remain forever. After much discussion, we'd decided it would be best to tell no one that Jack knew my secret. Not even Grandma, Aunt Lucy or the twins. I'd also promised that I would not use magic around Jack unless it was a matter of life and death.

What? Yes, of course I still used magic to clean the house. What could be more life and death than that? I just had to make sure Jack wasn't anywhere around when I did it.

***

After I'd checked my emails: all spam, and my post: all bills, I phoned Grandma, but there was no reply, so I set off in search of her. I started at Ever, which was as busy as usual.

"Hey, Julie, is my grandmother here?"

Julie was the head Everette; Grandma had taken her on not long after Kathy had left to set up her bridal shop. I really liked Julie; she had a wonderful personality: charming, polite and caring. I suppose she reminded me of myself.

What? Of course I have all those qualities and many more. Self-awareness and modesty to name just two.

Anyway, I was telling you about Julie. Apart from all the qualities that she and I shared, she had a wonderful way with Grandma. I'd never seen anyone who was able to handle her better. Nothing Grandma could say or do ever seemed to fluster Julie, who was coolness personified.

"Your grandmother isn't here, Jill. She popped in first thing, but then shot off again."

"I don't suppose she said where she was going?"

"Sorry, no. How long is it until the wedding now?"

"A week on Saturday."

"You're remarkably calm. I was a nervous wreck for weeks before I got married. There's so much to organise, isn't there?"

"I've got it all in hand."

"I'm very impressed."

"Thanks. I'd better let you get back to your customers."

Next stop: Ever A Wool Moment (or EAWM as I shall call it from now on). The reincarnation of Grandma's famous wool shop was across the road from its original base (now occupied by Ever). Just to rub Ma Chivers' nose in it, Grandma had built the new shop on the location previously occupied by Yarnstormers, which had mysteriously collapsed. The official reason given for that collapse had been old mine shafts, but one of my *moles* had told me otherwise.

All the old favourites were back on offer: the number of Everlasting Wool subscribers had exploded, and One-Size knitting needles were as popular as ever.

"Morning, Jill."

"Morning, Kim."

Kim Neaper was manager of EAWM. I'd first met her some time ago when she was working as a grim reaper, alongside my old friend, Jim Keeper. Kim had grown tired of the reaping business, mainly because she'd found it impossible to keep a boyfriend. What more logical career progression could there be than to go from grim reaper to manager of a wool shop?

"I'm looking for my grandmother. Is she here?"

"I haven't seen her yet today." She grinned. "Not that I'm complaining. Have you tried Ever?"

"I've just come from there. I guess that leaves only one place she can be. See you around, Kim."

"Hold on, Jill. How are the wedding plans going?"

Sheesh! Everywhere I went, it was all anyone wanted to talk about.

"Okay, thanks. Everything's under control. I'd better get going or her highness will give me grief."

"Bye, Jill."

Grandma was slowly but surely taking over Washbridge's retail sector. As well as EAWM and Ever on the high street, she also owned ForEver Bride on West Street—right next door to Kathy's Bridal Shop.

"Morning, Jill. Your grandmother has been looking for you." Eliza Domore was the manager of ForEver Bride. A nicer woman you couldn't hope to meet. What she'd done to deserve having to work for Grandma, goodness only knew.

"Morning, Eliza."

"There you are." Grandma appeared from the back of the shop. "Nice of you to bother."

"I've just spent the last ten minutes looking—"

"Never mind the excuses. Come through to my office." She turned and led the way to the back of the shop.

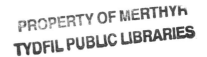

"You and that human of yours are going away on honeymoon, aren't you?"

"You know we are."

"Good. I'm going to need your house while you're away."

"Sorry?"

"Your house. I'm going to need it."

"Why?"

"For an old friend of mine, Madge Moleworthy. Have I mentioned her before?"

"I don't think so."

"Madge has never been to the human world before, but she has to come over here for a couple of weeks—something to do with her cousin. She needs somewhere to stay, and I said she could live at your house while you're away."

"Why can't she stay with her cousin?"

"They already have a house full."

"What's wrong with a hotel?"

"Madge is nervous enough about coming over here as it is. She'd never cope with a hotel."

"So, you thought you'd offer her our house?"

"Exactly. As luck would have it, her cousin lives only a couple of miles from your place, so it's ideal."

"And you didn't think you ought to ask me first?"

"Not really."

"I'm sorry, but it's simply not on."

"I've already promised her."

"You'll just have to un-promise her."

"I can't do that. And anyway, you owe me."

"What for?"

"For deciding to buy your wedding dress from next

door instead of from ForEver Bride."

"*Next door*, as you put it, belongs to my sister. Of course I chose Kathy over you."

"Which is precisely why you should do this for me. And Madge."

"What am I supposed to tell Jack?"

"Why do you have to tell that human anything?"

"Because it's his house too. If there's going to be a stranger living there, I think he has a right to know."

"Tell him the truth: that she's an old friend of mine. Come on, Jill. How often do I ask you to do anything for me?"

"All the time."

"Can I tell Madge it's okay?"

"I'll need to meet her first."

"Why?"

"Because you're asking me to allow a complete stranger to live in my house for a fortnight. I'm not going to agree to that until I've at least met the woman."

"Alright, if you insist. I'll set up a meeting with her."

"Okay."

"It's not long now until the big day."

"Don't you start going on about the wedding too. It's all anyone talks to me about."

"I'm not talking about your wedding. I'm talking about the launch of Ever A Wool Moment's app on Friday."

"You're launching an app?"

"I told you about it months ago."

"You tell me about a lot of things."

"It's going to revolutionise knitting."

"Really?" As if I cared.

"Just imagine. You're out and about, and you see

someone wearing a jumper that you like. You snap a photo using the app, and voila, it generates a pattern to create the garment."

"Sounds great." Yawn. "What have you called it?"

"Guess."

"I don't know. Copy Cat?"

"Nothing so boring. It's called: *See It. Make It*. Brilliant, eh?"

"Brilliant. Can I go now?"

"Yes. I'll let you know when I've arranged something with Madge."

"Wonderful."

Chapter 2

"Hey, traitor!" Kathy called to me as I passed by her shop. "I saw you sneaking out of next door."

"I wasn't sneaking. Grandma summoned me down here."

"It's a bit late for her to try to persuade you to buy your dress from her shop."

"It wasn't that, although I hope you appreciate all the flak I've had to take because I bought the dress from you."

"You're a martyr. Why did she drag you down here?"

"She wants to rent out our house while we're away on honeymoon."

"No way."

"Yes way. Well, not so much *rent* because we wouldn't actually get paid."

"To who?"

"One of her friends from Can—err—Canada."

"Your grandmother has friends who live in Canada?"

"Apparently. And Grandma has told her she can stay at our house while we're away."

"That was nice of her. No doubt she consulted with you first?"

"What do you think?"

"Don't forget about the final fitting for the dress."

"Yeah. Wednesday—I've got it in my diary."

"It's tomorrow night."

"Is it? I thought it was Wednesday."

"It's Tuesday. It's always been Tuesday. It's a good job I persuaded you to let Marceau plan this wedding, or it would never have happened."

"He's coming around again tonight. He practically lives

at our place."

"He's very thorough."

"That's one word for it. Apparently, we have to finalise the seating plan tonight."

"Good luck with that. I remember when Pete and I got married, there were more arguments about the seating plan than anything else."

"I don't get it. Why can't we just let everyone sit where they want?"

She rolled her eyes. "Like I said, it's a good thing you've got Marceau on the job."

I'd promised Aunt Lucy that I'd nip over to see Barry, who was going through a bit of a bad patch. His friend, Hamlet, had passed away two weeks earlier, and Barry still hadn't got over it.

First though, a caffeine-injection was called for.

I'd never really taken to Coffee Games, but the rebranding from Coffee Triangle had obviously been a success; the place was much busier since the change.

I'd never liked games, and especially not board games. When I was a kid, I always dreaded that period, just after we'd eaten Christmas dinner, when everyone wanted to play stupid board games. Monopoly was about the only one I could stand, and that was only because I used to cheat by stealing cash out of the bank.

What? Everyone does that. Don't they?

In the same way as Coffee Triangle used to have an instrument of the day, Coffee Games now had a game of the day. And judging by the weird buzzing noises coming from around the shop, today was 'Operation' day. It was just as well that I'd never wanted to embark on a medical career because I'd always been useless at that stupid game. Except for that one time when I'd beaten Mum, Dad and Kathy, but that might have been because I'd sneakily disconnected the battery. Snigger.

There was a familiar face behind the counter.

"Blaze?"

"Hi, Jill. Long time, no see."

"Is Daze here?"

"Haven't you heard? I've been promoted. I'm working solo now."

"Congratulations. Are you enjoying it?"

"It's a bit nerve racking, but it definitely has some advantages." After checking that no one was watching, he undid one of the buttons on his shirt, to reveal a luminous orange catsuit underneath.

"Wow!" I laughed. "I don't think Daze would have approved of that."

"She'd have been apoplectic with rage."

"Is she working solo now, too?"

"No, she's got a new partner, but from what I've heard, he's pretty useless. What can I get for you, Jill?"

"A caramel latte, and one of those blueberry muffins, please."

"Would you like a board game?"

"Operation? No, I hate that game."

"Really? It's one of my favourites. I reached the semi-finals of the Candlefield Operation Tournament last year."

"Please tell me that's not really a thing."

"It really is. And, I came sixth at Kerplunk the year before."

"Very impressive." I glanced around to make sure no one could overhear. "I assume you're here undercover?"

"Yeah. We've had reports that some vampires are trying to establish a 'blood distribution network' here in Washbridge."

"Human blood?"

"That's right. They approach established businesses run by vampires and try to persuade them to carry supplies of the blood. Their favourite targets are coffee shops, bars and clubs. I'm hoping to catch them red-handed."

"I didn't realise that the owner of this place was a vampire."

"Rodney? Yeah, he bought the place just over a year ago. It was his idea to change the theme from percussion to board games. You might not have seen him, though, because he rarely comes out during the day."

"How exactly do they operate this blood distribution network?"

"They provide the shop, bar or club with a fridge, designed to look like a safe, and then deliver fresh supplies of blood several times a week. We've closed down a few outlets already, but what we're really after is the people behind the network, so we can shut down the operation altogether."

"Is Daze working on that too?"

"No. I'm not sure what she's doing at the moment."

The coffee and muffin had certainly hit the mark, but I was glad to get back outside, away from the constant buzzing of the games. I was just about to magic myself over to Candlefield when someone called my name. It was the unmistakeable dulcet tones of Deli.

"Jill!" She was across the road, standing in the doorway of Nailed-It. The nail bar had been forced to relocate when

I-Sweat gave up their lease.

"Morning, Deli." I walked over to her.

"I was going to come up and see you later, Jill. You've saved me a trip. Mad called last night to say she'll be coming up on Thursday, in time for the hen night. She asked me to let you know."

"That's great."

Mad had already confirmed she was coming to the wedding, but she hadn't been sure if she'd be able to make it to the hen night.

"Where's she going to stay?"

"With us of course. She was going to book a hotel, but I wouldn't hear of it. I can't wait to see her again."

"Me neither. It's been very quiet without her."

"You must be getting nervous, Jill. It won't be long now."

"I'm okay. Jack's nervous enough for both of us." I glanced through the shop window. "How's business? It looks like you're busy."

"It's going really well, thanks. Especially since I got up to speed."

"Are you and Nails both doing the nails now?"

"Yeah, but most people still ask for him. We've put up his rates—he now charges twice as much as I do. Hopefully, the price hike will persuade a few people to give me a go. Hey, I've just had a brilliant idea."

Oh dear.

"I could do your nails for the wedding."

"Err—I—err—thanks, but—"

"I wouldn't charge you anything. It would be part of my wedding gift. Please, Jill, it would mean a lot to me."

"Are you sure you—err—that's to say, do you know

what you're—I mean, are you definitely okay working on *real* hands?"

"Oh yeah. Defo. I could do them for you on the day before the wedding. What do you say?"

"Okay then. I guess it would be nice to have attractive nails for a change."

"Great. I'll see you on the hen night."

***

Aunt Lucy had now settled into her new home. Everything was pretty much perfect except for her next-door neighbour: Grandma.

"Hi, Jill." She was baking what looked like cupcakes.

"Morning. Are you enjoying your day off?"

"It doesn't seem right to call it that, but it is nice to have some time to myself."

Aunt Lucy looked after Amber's little girl, Lil, on Tuesdays and Thursdays, and then Pearl's little girl, Lil, on Wednesdays and Fridays. That arrangement allowed the twins to keep working at Cuppy C, two days each, every week.

Yes, you did hear right. Neither Amber nor Pearl would back down, so now Aunt Lucy had two granddaughters, both named Lil.

"Where's Barry?"

"In the back garden."

"Is he any better?"

"Not really. He didn't even want to go for a walk yesterday."

"That's not a good sign. I'll see if I can cheer him up."

"Good luck. Do you want a drink?"

"No, thanks. I've just had a coffee."

When Aunt Lucy had moved into her new house, the back garden had been overrun with weeds. The previous occupant, an elderly witch, had found the upkeep too much for her towards the end. Now though, it was back to its former glory—thanks to the long hours put in by Aunt Lucy, ably assisted by Lester.

Barry was lying on the path, staring out of the gate. Normally, when I came to see him, he was all over me like a rash, but since Hamlet's death, he'd been much more subdued.

"Hi, Barry."

"Hello."

"How are you?"

"Okay."

"Are you sure? You don't look very happy."

"I miss Hamlet."

"We all do, but he wouldn't want you to be sad, would he?"

"I can't help it."

"I've had an idea. Why don't we see if we can get you another hamster?"

"It wouldn't be Hamlet."

"I know, but—"

"I don't want another hamster."

"Okay, that's understandable. How about we go to Everything Rodent to see if they have any other pets you might like."

"What kind of pet?"

"I don't know. Why don't we see what they have? What do you say?"

"Okay, I guess."

"Great. Come on, then. There's no time like the present."

***

Bill Ratman was behind the counter in Everything Rodent.

"Morning, you two. I heard about Hamlet. My condolences to both of you."

"Thanks, Bill. I thought we might get Barry another pet."

"Another hamster?"

"No!" Barry said. "Don't want a hamster."

"Of course. I understand. What did you have in mind?"

"We're open to suggestions," I said. "In your experience, what would make the best pet for a dog?"

"After hamsters? I'd say tortoises."

"That sounds like a great idea. What do you think, Barry?"

"They have shells." He perked up for the first time that morning. "I like shells."

"A tortoise it is, then." I looked around. "Where are they?"

"Tortoises aren't rodents."

"Of course. Silly me. Any idea where we might get one?"

"You need Everything Reptile. It's owned by my cousin, Truman."

"Your cousin? Pets really do run in your family, don't they?"

"Truman actually opened his shop first. In fact, he was the inspiration for me to open this place."

Before we left, Bill gave Barry a handful of Barkies, which I was pleased to see he devoured enthusiastically.

"What do tortoises eat?" Barry asked, as we walked to Everything Reptile.

"I'm not sure."

"Do they like Barkies?"

"I doubt it. I think they prefer leaves."

"Yuk. Barkies are much better."

Everything Reptile was deserted.

"Hello? Anyone in?" I shouted from the counter.

"Just a moment. I'm cleaning out the geckos." The voice came from the room behind the counter.

"What's a gecko, Jill?" Barry said.

"A kind of lizard, I think."

"You're correct." A man appeared behind the counter. "Sorry to keep you waiting."

"Are you Truman?"

"That's me. Truman Turtle at your service."

"Turtle?" I laughed.

He didn't.

"Sorry. Your cousin, Bill Ratman, suggested that we pay you a visit. I'm looking for a pet for Barry. Bill suggested a tortoise."

"Tortoises are ideal companions for dogs."

"What are those?" Barry pulled me across the shop.

"They look like baby crocodiles. I shouldn't get too close."

"I like these." He stuck his nose even closer.

"Barry, don't—"

"Ouch!" He jumped back. "It bit me."

"Let me look. It's okay. It didn't break the skin."

"I don't like crocodiles." He backed away.

"I'm pleased to hear that. Let's go and check out the tortoises."

While Barry had been investigating the crocodiles, Truman had been in the back room to get a tortoise.

"There's been something of a run on tortoises over the last few days. This guy is the only one I have left."

"I like him." Barry's tail was wagging like crazy. "Can I have him, Jill? Please?"

"Sure. Why not?"

Whilst I had no wish to speak ill of the dead, Hamlet had been quite a demanding rodent—he'd run me ragged at times. At least with a tortoise, I could look forward to a quiet life. So far, this one hadn't even popped his head out of his shell—he was probably fast asleep.

I paid and was just about to leave the shop when it occurred to me that I didn't know the tortoise's name.

"Excuse me, Truman. What's his name?"

Before he could answer, his phone rang.

"Everything Reptile. Truman speaking. How can I help?" He turned to me and mouthed the name.

"What is it?" Barry asked.

"I think he said it's Dimes."

After dropping Barry, and his new friend, back at Aunt Lucy's house, I phoned Mrs V to see if there had been any messages. There hadn't, and as I had no live cases, I decided to give myself the rest of the day off. At least, that way I'd have a little time to myself before Marceau arrived.

***

I hadn't seen Mr Ivers in the toll booth for ages, and curiosity had finally got the better of me.

"Doesn't Mr Ivers work here anymore?"

"Didn't you hear?" The young man was obviously trying to grow a moustache, but with limited success.

"Hear what?"

"Ivers won the lottery. Jammy sod."

"Really? When was that?"

"A couple of months back. He didn't win the jackpot, but from what I heard, he cleared almost half a mil. Wish it had been me."

"Me too."

There was no justice in the world. Why couldn't I win the lottery?

What? Yes, I do realise that I never buy a ticket, but that's not the point, is it? It's the principle that counts. Some people—me for example—are simply more deserving. That's all I'm saying.

I'd only driven half-a-mile from the bridge when I noticed two people, dressed in overalls, by the side of the road—they appeared to be pruning back the bushes. As I got closer, I recognised one of them, so I pulled up a little further up the road and walked back.

"Daze?"

"Hi, Jill."

"I see you've got a new sidekick." I gestured to the young man a few metres away.

"Don't remind me. Laze is a total waste of space."

"*Laze*? Is that his name?"

"No, it's just what I call him because he's so lazy."

"I saw Blaze earlier in Coffee Games."

"I bet he was wearing a luminous cat suit, wasn't he?" She grinned.

"Orange. It was horrible."

"Oh well. He's not my problem now, so he can do what he likes. Don't tell him that I said this, but he's turned out to be a great rogue retriever, which is more than this lazy oaf will ever do."

"What are you doing in my neck of the woods?"

"Actually, we're working on a really interesting case."

"Tell me more."

"According to our intel, there's a witch who lives hereabouts who's told her human partner that she's a sup."

"Oh?" Gulp.

"And from what we understand, they're due to get married, Saturday after next."

Oh bum! The game was up.

"I—err—I—"

"You should see your face." She laughed. "It's a picture."

"How did you know?"

"I didn't. At least, I wasn't sure until just now when I saw your reaction."

"You were bluffing?"

"Good, aren't I?"

"What are you going to do?"

"Don't worry. You're safe."

"Really?"

"By rights, I should take you back to Candlefield, and make sure you never leave again, but if anyone ever deserved a free pass, it's you. I've lost track of the number of times you've been there for me. And anyway, I've already bought my dress for the wedding. You don't think I'm going to waste that, do you?"

"How long have you suspected?"

"Ever since you told me you were getting married. I know you well enough to know you wouldn't go into this without first coming clean to Jack. How did he take it?"

"He was in a state of shock for a long time, but he's just about got used to it now."

"Does anyone else know that he knows?"

"No. I haven't told anyone."

"Not even your grandmother?"

"Especially not her."

"Good. You need to keep it that way. And make sure Jack understands that too because if it was ever to get out, I'd have no choice but to — well, you know."

"I understand. Thanks, Daze." I gave her a hug. "Are you sure you won't come on the hen night?"

"Thanks, but it's not really my scene. Incidentally, is the music festival going to cause you any problems?"

"What music festival?"

"You must have seen all the posters — they're everywhere. It's on the same day as your wedding — in Washbridge Park."

"Jack and Marceau haven't mentioned it, so I assume they don't think it will be a problem."

"Who's Marceau?"

"Our wedding planner and the bane of my life."

"My clippers have broken!" Laze shouted.

"Sorry, Jill. I'd better go and see to dumb-nuts."

Chapter 3

By the time I got up the next morning, Jack was already in the kitchen, eating breakfast.

"Morning." I managed between yawns.

"Morning, Gorgeous." He gave me a muesli kiss. "How's your head this morning?"

"My head?"

"Did the migraine go off last night?"

"Oh, right. Yeah, it's fine, thanks."

The previous evening, I'd managed to put up with two hours of Jack and Marceau, arranging and then rearranging the seating plan, but then it had got to a point where I couldn't stand anymore, so I'd made the excuse that I had a migraine, and left them to it. It wasn't an out and out lie—the whole thing was certainly giving me one.

"I'm pleased to report that we managed to finalise the seating plan last night," he said.

"Great."

"Well, almost."

"What do you mean: *almost*?"

"You have to admit that we have some unusual issues to address."

"Such as?"

"It can't be everyone who has to accommodate ghosts in their planning."

"You didn't mention ghosts to Marceau, did you?"

"Of course not. He would have thought I was crazy. But the fact that I can't tell him is half the problem. He can't understand why I insist on having one table more than the official guest list dictates we need."

"How did you explain that away?"

"I said we might make some last-minute additions to the guest list, so we wanted an extra table, just in case."

"Very clever. I'm impressed."

"It still leaves us with a slight problem, though."

"Oh?"

"I know you said that you wanted your mum and dad, and their partners to sit as close to the top table as possible, but there was no way I could convince Marceau that we should have what he thinks is an empty table positioned there. I had to agree to having it at the back of the room."

"That makes sense. I'll just have to explain it to Mum and Dad."

"While we're on the subject, we need to talk about the seating at the ceremony itself."

"What about it?"

"Your mum and dad will have to sit at the back there too."

"Why?"

"Think about it. If they sit near the front, those seats will appear to be empty to everyone except you. Someone will end up sitting on their laps."

Oh bum! I hadn't thought about that.

"You're right. I'll just have to try to explain it to them."

"Surely, they'll understand, won't they?"

"I wouldn't bank on it, but that's my problem. There's something else you need to know. I couldn't tell you last night because Marceau was here. On my way home, I bumped into Daze. You remember her, don't you?"

"Isn't she one of those rogue retainers you told me about?"

"Retrievers, but yeah. That's her. She knows."

"She knows what?"

"She knows that you know."

"Are you sure you don't still have a migraine? You aren't making a lick of sense."

"Daze knows that you know I'm a witch."

"What?" He dropped his spoon onto the floor. "Why didn't you tell me last night? What's going to happen? Is she going to take you—"

"Whoa, it's okay. I didn't say anything last night because Marceau was here, but also because Daze isn't going to do anything."

"How come? I thought that was her job."

"It is. She's going out on a limb for us. It's a big risk because if anyone finds out, she'll be in serious trouble."

"Are you sure you can trust her?"

"Absolutely. She made me promise I wouldn't tell you that she knew, but I'm not prepared to keep any more secrets from you ever again. Whatever you do, you mustn't let on that you know that she knows."

"Let me get this straight. I can't let her know that I know that she knows?

"Precisely. It's really important, Jack. If she finds out that I've told you—"

"She won't. Look, if I can keep your *big* secret, I'm sure I can manage this. How did she find out, anyway?"

"Daze is a smart cookie. She knew I wouldn't have agreed to marry you without first telling you I was a witch. Although, to be honest, she hadn't been one-hundred percent certain until she saw my reaction when she confronted me. She totally bluffed me."

Jack had finished his breakfast, and gone through to the

lounge, to catch up on the morning's bowling news on TenPin TV. I was still trying to decide between toast and cornflakes when he called to me.

"It looks like someone is moving in next door."

A removal van had pulled onto the driveway of what had, until a couple of months earlier, been Megan Love's house. I'd grown to like Megan, and had been sad to see her leave when she moved in with her boyfriend, Ryan. There had been other comings and goings on the street too. Two adjoining houses across the road had become vacant at pretty much the same time. One had belonged to Blossom, AKA The Rose, who had disappeared after her failed attempt to kill me had resulted in the death of Jack's mother. The other house had been occupied by the balaclava twins who had turned out to be the famous artists: Chris and Chrissie Chrisling—better known as Chris To The Power Of Three. They had used the house as a base in which to create their next masterpiece—a pile of buckets all stuck together.

Would-be house-buyers seemed to have been put off by the two adjoining vacant properties—they probably suspected there was some kind of structural issue. After standing empty for almost a year, one of the houses had been bought about a month ago by a middle-aged couple who I had yet to meet. According to Jack, they'd told him that they were 'something in showbusiness'. Someone had finally moved into the adjacent property only last week, but we hadn't seen hide nor hair of them yet. And now, it seemed we had a new next-door neighbour.

"Have you seen who it is?" I said.

Jack shook his head. "So far, I've only seen the removal men. They must have the keys because they've started taking stuff inside. Let's hope our new next-door neighbours aren't as crazy as those on the other side."

"Tony and Clare are okay."

"They're nice enough, but you do have to worry about a couple who spend most of their time dressed in weird costumes."

"That's not what you said the other night in bed when you suggested I should wear —"

"That's totally different." He interrupted. "Over the last few weeks alone, I've bumped into giant fish, telephones and hammers. You have to admit that's a bit weird."

"There's nothing wrong with being weird. At least they aren't boring. Mind you, this time last year, my money would have been on them moving out."

"You mean when they almost split up because of Tony's fling with a broad bean?"

"It was a runner bean, but yeah. I thought they were done for until they made up at CupidCon."

"I haven't seen them yet this week. Maybe they don't have a con for once."

"I wouldn't bet on it."

While Jack was getting changed upstairs, I continued to ponder the toast/cornflakes conundrum. I was still undecided when he came back down.

"You don't seem to be in any hurry this morning." He grinned. "Don't you have much work on at the moment?"

"I'm still trying to decide what to have for breakfast. These decisions can't be rushed."

"Apparently not."

"But in answer to your question, business is a little slow at the moment. I am going to CASS later, though."

"I'd forgotten it was your day to be 'Teach'. Do the kids bring 'Miss' an apple?"

"One of them did bring me a bun last week. He'd baked it himself, and it was pretty awful."

"I hope you didn't tell him that."

"Of course I didn't. Just how tactless do you think I am? Don't answer that."

"I envy you being able to magic yourself to a completely different world."

"I've told you before. Candlefield isn't that much different to here."

"CASS sounds really cool, though. A castle in the middle of nowhere, surrounded by dragons and all manner of strange creatures — that has to be exciting."

"CASS is great, but I'm never there long enough to appreciate it fully."

"I suppose I'd better get going. Have a good day, and don't forget you have to go for the final dress fitting tonight."

"I don't see why I need to. It fit perfectly well the last time I tried it on."

"If you don't, Kathy will kill you. And don't forget that I'm going bowling straight after work."

Decision made. Cornflakes it was.

I always looked forward to my days at CASS. It had all started over a year ago when the headmistress had asked me to give a talk to the kids. That had been postponed when a pouchfeeder had snatched one of the younger pupils. Months later, when I'd eventually delivered my talk, I'd been incredibly nervous, but it had gone down really well. So well, in fact, that the headmistress had asked if I'd be prepared to hold regular classes on The Human World.

At first, I said no, but Desdemona Nightowl wasn't one to give up easily. She'd kept on at me until I caved in and agreed to teach a class every couple of weeks. I say 'teach', but they weren't really lessons because there was no fixed curriculum and no examinations. I was simply there to talk to the kids about the human world, and to answer any questions they might have. I took classes of all ages, from the nervous first years through to those about to graduate. Usually, it was fun, although there were a few kids who tried to give me the run around. While it was nice to get away from the rigours of being a private investigator, I had no plans to become a full-time teacher. That would have meant doing real work—no thank you.

***

When I arrived at my office building, a wizard held the door open for me.

"After you," he said.

"Thanks."

"Do you work here?" He was tall, and good-looking in a boy-band kind of way.

"Yeah. I'm Jill Gooder. Those are my offices at the top of the stairs, on the right. Were you on your way to see me?"

"Actually no. I'm Lucas Morecake. My partner, Wendy, and I have taken over the units just down the corridor from you, including the one that used to be a gym."

"Right. I saw your sign. Escape? What is that? A travel agent's?"

"No. Escape rooms."

"Sorry? What?"

"Haven't you heard of them? They're all the rage, particularly in the large cities. Ours will be the first in Washbridge."

"What exactly is an escape room?"

"It's a sort of adventure game. You have to follow the clues and solve the riddles to complete the task."

"And people pay to do that?"

"Quite handsomely, I'm pleased to say. You must come and check us out once we're open for business."

"When will that be?"

"Within a couple of weeks, hopefully."

"Well, I wish you the best of luck."

"Thanks, but I don't think we'll have to rely on luck because we have a secret weapon." He winked at me.

"How do you mean?"

"The problem with most escape rooms is they have only a few different themes—sometimes just one or two. Once a customer has tried all the different themed rooms, there's no reason for them to return. We won't have that problem. We can offer our customers an infinite selection of different rooms and themes."

"How can you do that? Hold on—are you talking about using magic?"

He grinned. "Nice to meet you, Jill. I'd better get going. Wendy and I are due to meet with our accountant in a few minutes."

This wasn't good news. It sounded as though Lucas and his partner intended to use magic to power the escape rooms. Unless they were very careful, that might attract some unwanted attention from the human press, and if that happened, I'd be a little too close to their operations for comfort.

There was no sign of Mrs V in the outer office where the tripwire was still straddling the room. I considered doing the limbo under it, but I didn't want to risk injuring my back, so I stepped over it instead.

When I went through to my office, I found Mrs V in there. She was deep in conversation with a man who was wearing his hair in a ponytail. Neither of them seemed to notice my arrival, so I cleared my throat to catch their attention.

"Jill, I didn't hear you come in," Mrs V said. "This is Brian Briggs. I told you about him."

"The Feng Shui guy."

"Grandmaster."

"Of course."

"Pleased to make your acquaintance, Jill." He stepped forward and offered his hand. He had a grip like a wet lettuce.

"You too. Mrs V seems pleased with the work you've done for her."

"Brian just dropped in to see how I was getting on," Mrs V said. "I asked him to take a look at your office while he was here."

"Oh?"

"The news isn't good." Brian frowned. "The energy is all wrong."

"Brian has said he can sort it out for you, Jill." Mrs V was clearly a fangirl.

"There would of course be a small fee," Brian said.

"How small?"

"My usual consultation fee is five-hundred pounds."

"What?" I turned to Mrs V. "Is that how much you paid?"

"No. My room is smaller and there's less furniture. It was only three-hundred pounds. It's well worth it, Jill. My knitting speed has doubled since the changes."

"As luck would have it," Brian chipped in. "I have a couple of free slots next week."

"Right. I'll have to think about it."

"Of course. Here's my card. My number is on there."

"Great. Thanks very much."

I waited until Mrs V had led Brian out of my office, then I ripped the business card into pieces and dropped them in the bin.

"You should get in on that scam." Winky appeared from under the sofa.

"What scam?"

"Feng whatty. You should set yourself up as an expert."

"Grandmaster."

"Whatever. Get some cards printed and off you go."

"I don't know anything about Feng Shui."

"What does that matter? Just shuffle the furniture around a bit and then collect the cash."

"That would hardly be ethical."

"You're thinking about it—I can tell you are."

"Of course I'm not. I do have some scruples you know."

"Since when?"

Twenty minutes later, I was still weighing up the pros and cons of becoming a Feng Shui grandmaster when a phone rang.

It wasn't mine.

"Judy, my little darling," Winky said. "All the better for hearing your voice. It feels like ages since I saw you. Is it really only yesterday? That just shows how much I've missed you. Tonight? Yes, of course. Your place or mine? Okay, I'll see you then." He blew a few kisses down the phone and then ended the call.

"Judy?" I said.

"You shouldn't be listening to my calls."

"It's hard not to. And anyway, I thought you were seeing Daisy? You were on the phone to her on Friday."

"I am seeing Daisy."

"What about Judy?"

"I'm seeing her too. And Trixie."

"You can't do that."

"Why not? I'm young, free and single now. I can see whoever I like."

"Yes, but not at the same time. Do they know about one another?"

"What do you think?" He grinned.

Even though I didn't approve of his three-timing, it was good to see Winky back to his old self. He'd been devastated when Peggy had left. Her owners (not a term he would agree with), had upped and moved to the other end of the country. Peggy hadn't known it was coming, and she'd been as torn up about it as Winky. Watching them say their last goodbyes had brought tears to my eyes.

What? It's true. Deep down, I'm just an old softy.

After Peggy had left, Winky had been down in the dumps for a long time, but now he'd bounced back with a vengeance.

Chapter 4

Rather than magicking myself directly to CASS, I decided to call in at Cuppy C first. Pearl and Mindy were behind the tea room counter.

Just before they'd left to have their babies, the twins had taken on Mindy as a fulltime assistant. Although Mindy had once been persona non-grata, it was now generally accepted that she'd been acting under the influence of Miles Best, her very much ex-boyfriend. Since dumping that loser, Mindy had been an all-round much nicer person. Plus, she had the experience of working in a cake shop and tea room, which she'd gained working in Best Cakes.

"Blueberry muffin, Jill?" Mindy greeted me with a smile.

"I'll just take a caramel latte, please."

"Aren't you feeling well?" Pearl quipped.

"I'm on my way to CASS in a few minutes. They always have a good supply of biscuits and cakes in the staff room, and they're all free."

"Cheapskate." Pearl laughed. "How come you've dropped in here for coffee if that's free over there too?"

"To see you, of course."

"And the real reason?"

"The coffee over at CASS is pretty ropey."

"There you are." Mindy handed me the coffee, and then went to serve the next customer.

"Let's have a quick chinwag." Pearl gestured to the table nearest to the counter. "I can nip back if we get busy."

"How's Lil?" I said.

"Beautiful as always. I don't like to say anything in case I upset Amber, but my Lil is so much prettier than her Lil, don't you think?"

"I—err—they're both beautiful."

"It's okay, Jill, I realise you have to say that. It's true, though, my Lil is so much more attractive."

"How's being here part-time working out?"

"Okay. It's nice to get out of the house, and I enjoy chatting to the customers, but I miss Lil something awful."

"It's only a few hours, a couple of days a week, though. And you know she'll be okay with Aunt Lucy."

"Yeah, Mum's great with her, but then Lil is so well behaved—you barely hear a peep out of her. I feel sorry for Mum having to look after Amber's Lil, though. She cries all the time."

"How is Mindy doing?"

"Great. Amber and I had our reservations at first, but she's proven to be worth her weight in gold. Don't say anything to her, but we're thinking of making her the manager. She's practically acting as one already, particularly on the days when we're not here." Pearl glanced across at the counter where a queue was starting to form. "I'd better get back to work. Have a good day at CASS."

***

I was the only one able to magic myself back and forth between Candlefield and CASS. Everyone else was forced to travel on the airship. That's why I always made a point of magicking myself to the same quiet corner of the west wing where no one would see me arrive. That way, I didn't rub everyone's nose in it.

The staffroom was two floors below my landing spot, and always my first port of call before going to my class.

"Morning, Jill," Reginald Crowe was seated in his favourite chair, right by the door.

"Morning, Reggie. That looks nice." I gestured to the half-eaten muffin on his plate.

"It's delicious. Highly recommended."

Reggie was the school's caretaker and general handyman. I'd originally met him on the airship on my first ever visit to CASS. On that occasion, he'd helped to calm my nerves about the flight, and since then, he'd become a firm friend. It had to be said, though, that he seemed to spend more time in the staff room than he did working.

As always, there was a fabulous spread of scrumptious cakes. I had no idea who paid for them, but they were all free to the staff, and that was good enough for me. I didn't get paid for teaching at CASS, so I considered the cakes to be payment-in-kind.

"Morning, Jill."

"Morning, Mrs Eastwest."

"I do wish you'd call me Phil."

I just couldn't bring myself to call Philomena Eastwest anything other than Mrs Eastwest. It would have been like calling Mrs V, Annabel. Mrs Eastwest was a thousand years old, or at least she looked it. Even so, she seemed to have boundless energy. When I'd first met her, I'd assumed she taught English, History or something similar. It turned out she was the P.E. teacher. In her youth, she'd apparently been a top track and field athlete. Today, her frail body meant she wasn't able to participate in physical activities, but that didn't stop her barking out orders to the kids. Her body might be failing her, but her mind was laser sharp. I'd sat in on one of her P.E. sessions, and she hadn't missed a thing. When any of the kids slacked off, Mrs Eastwest was quickly on their case.

"Aren't you having a bun, Mrs Eastwest?"

"Certainly not. It's strictly fruit for me between meals."

"Me too."

She looked at the muffin I'd just put onto my plate.

"It's blueberry," I offered in my defence.

"How are you enjoying working at CASS? It must be rather boring compared to your main job?"

"I enjoy it. The kids keep me on my toes."

"I bet. Which class are you taking today?"

"Some of the first-years. Class one-alpha."

"The first-years are the best. At that age, they're still nervous, and respectful of the staff, but that doesn't last long. Just be sure to watch out for Fleabert Junior."

"I don't recall anyone by that name."

"He was here for the start of term, but then got called home for some reason. Apparently, it related to some incident in the human world. I don't know the details, but I believe the rogue retrievers were involved."

"Surely, it couldn't have been anything he did, could it? He's only what, thirteen?"

"You may change your mind when you meet him. I taught his father, Fleabert Senior. The man was, and still is, a colossal pain in the bum."

"Right, thanks for the heads-up."

"I must be making tracks." She put down her cup. "I need to do an inventory of the skipping ropes before next week's inter-house sports competition. I assume you'll be attending?"

"I'd love to but I'm going to be rather busy on that day."

"What could possibly be more important than the inter-house sports competition?"

"I get married the next day."

"Really? Congratulations. I suppose I'm the last to hear; I usually am. I guess that does take priority over our little competition." She smiled.

I finished off the muffin and was considering helping myself to a second one when someone grabbed me by the arm.

"Have you heard the rumour, Jill?" It was Natasha Fastjersey, the head librarian.

"What's that?"

"You didn't hear this from me, but the word is that the headmistress intends to retire."

"Are you sure? She hasn't been here very long."

"Health reasons. That's what I heard."

"She seemed perfectly fine when I was here last."

"She still does, but one can never tell, can one? Anyway, not a word to anyone."

"Of course not."

Could the headmistress really be planning to retire? I certainly hoped not—Desdemona Nightowl represented everything that was good about CASS. I for one would be sorry to see her go. Maybe, Natasha had got it wrong—it wouldn't be the first time. She'd once told me that she'd heard the airships were being replaced by giant catapults, which would be used to propel people between CASS and Candlefield. She'd failed to realise what the date was.

Some of the pupils had fed her that information via the CASS newsletter which just happened to be dated 1st April.

***

Even though I'd been teaching for several months, my nerves still began to jangle every time I stepped into the classroom. I would rather have faced down a hardened criminal in my 'real' job than face a classroom full of kids, even though for the most part they were well behaved.

Although the kids didn't refer to me as 'Teacher', they were required to call me Miss Gooder. I'd told the headmistress that I'd prefer they called me Jill, but she insisted that would set an unacceptable precedent. I wouldn't be Miss Gooder for much longer, though. Jack and I had had several long conversations on the subject of my name. He'd suggested I might want to keep 'Gooder' after we were married — if for no other reason than for the business. I'd given it careful consideration, but in the end, I'd decided that I would take his name. That meant I'd be Jill Gooder for only a few more days, and then I'd become Jill Maxwell. It would take some getting used to, and I'd have to buy a new sign for the office, but on balance I thought it was the right decision.

"Morning, Miss Gooder," the kids all chorused when I entered the classroom.

"Morning, class one-alpha. Please take your seats."

As I glanced around, I spotted a new face seated in the back row, close to the window. I assumed it must be Fleabert Junior. To look at him, it seemed like butter wouldn't melt, but I knew I had better heed Mrs

Eastwest's words of warning.

"Right, everyone, I thought today we could talk about the internet. Have any of you heard of that?"

A few hands went up. One of them belonged to Fleabert Junior.

I pointed to him. "I haven't seen you in my class before. What's your name?"

"Randall Fleabert Junior, Miss. I had to return home for a few weeks."

"Why is that?"

"I had to appear in youth court back in the human world because I'd got into a spot of bother."

"What happened?"

"It was my parents' fault. They were the ones who wanted to drag me to this dump. I didn't want to come, so I lost my temper, and broke a few things."

"What kind of things?"

"The windows of the police station."

"What good did you think that would do?"

"I thought if I could get arrested, my parents wouldn't be able to send me to CASS, and that I'd be able to stay in the human world."

"I take it that things didn't work out as you'd planned."

"They let me off with a fine and a slapped wrist."

"Well you're here now, so what can you tell us about the internet?"

"It's brilliant. There's all sorts on there: Snapchat, Facebook, Instagram, everything. I used to spend all day online. I hate it here—it's so boring without it."

"I'm not sure it's a good idea to spend all day online, but if any of you are considering visiting the human world, or even working there eventually, it's as well you're aware of the internet because it plays a major part in many aspects of human life."

"I'd got sixty followers on Twitter!" Fleabert blurted out.

"That's very nice, but there are much more important uses for the internet, and I intend to discuss some of those today."

My first few lessons had been a bit of a disaster because I'd tried to run them by the seat of my pants. I'd soon realised that I needed to prepare notes ahead of the lesson. Nothing too detailed—just a basic structure. Quite often, the conversations would drift away from the plan, but that was okay.

The kids generally seemed excited about the internet, particularly those who had yet to visit the human world.

"Ouch!" Lucinda Blade touched her ear.

"What's wrong, Lucinda?"

"Something hurt me, Miss."

"Have you been stung?"

"I don't think so."

"Are you alright?"

"Yes, Miss."

"Okay, let's carry on."

Five minutes later, Ruby Noonday called out in pain. "Miss! Something pinched my arm."

"Are you okay?"

"I think so."

Something weird was going on. I was fairly certain that it wasn't a wasp or a bee because the girls had been able to shrug it off so easily. Everyone in the room looked nervous, in case it was their turn to be 'stung' next.

Everyone that is except for Fleabert Junior. He was grinning from ear to ear.

As the class discussion continued, I kept one eye on Fleabert. Five minutes later, I noticed something: Although he was doing his best to hide it, he was casting an unusual combination of spells. It took me a few seconds, but I was able to decode them just in time. As soon as I had, I quickly reversed both of his spells.

"Ouch!" Sally Topps screamed.

"Mr Fleabert!" I shouted. "What are you doing?"

Everyone was staring at Fleabert who was standing next to Sally Topps' desk.

"I—err—how?" he spluttered.

"You're obviously a talented wizard, Mr Fleabert. It's just a pity that you don't put your magic to better use."

"How did you know?"

"That you'd used the 'copy' spell to leave an image of yourself in the chair, and then the 'invisible' spell that allowed you to move around the room undetected? It wasn't difficult."

"No one else has ever worked it out."

"This is Jill Gooder, Dumbo," Sally Topps said. "She's the most powerful witch in Candlefield." She turned to me. "Sorry for calling you by your first name, Miss."

"That's alright, Sally. Now, Mr Fleabert, I think an hour's detention after school would be in order, don't you?"

"But, Miss, it's sports practice."

"Not for you, I'm afraid. You can write me an essay on the dangers of social media."

"But, Miss, I don't know anything about social media."

"Didn't you say how much you like Snapchat, Facebook

and Instagram? And then there's your sixty followers on Twitter. It seems to me that you're very well acquainted with social media. Now, get back to your seat."

Ten minutes from the end of the lesson, I threw open the floor for questions.

Destiny Braden's hand flew up first.

"Yes, Destiny?"

"Is it true you're getting married the weekend after next, Miss?"

"I'm not sure that comes under the heading of human studies."

"But, Miss, aren't you going to marry a human?"

"Actually, you're right on both counts. I'm getting married a week on Saturday to Jack who is a human."

"Isn't it kind of weird living with a human?" Johnny Linkfur shouted.

"Not at all. Humans aren't very different from us. In fact, for those of you who don't already know, I was raised in a family of humans, and thought I was human until just a few years ago."

"Miss!" Charlie Hedges raised his hand.

"Yes, Charlie."

"Who do you want to win the inter-house sports competition?"

"That definitely doesn't come under the heading of human studies."

"Come on, Miss. Who will you be shouting for?"

"The competition is actually on the day before I get married, so I won't be able to make it. I'll have enough on my plate that day, so I can't afford any distractions. I wish all the teams the best of luck."

"Wrongacre will win easily, Miss!"

"Rubbish. Nomad are unbeatable."

"Longstaff forever!"

"Capstan's name is already on the cup!"

I was surprised at just how enthusiastic all the kids seemed to be about the upcoming sports competition. When I'd been at school, I'd done everything I could to avoid taking part in sports day. Needless to say, Kathy had been star of both track and field. And of course, she'd taken every opportunity to rub my nose in it.

"Okay, kids. That's it for today. See you next time. Mr Fleabert, make sure you drop the essay into the staff room this evening after detention. I'll tell Mrs Eastwest to expect it."

The kids all filed out of the classroom; Beth Nightling was the last to leave.

"Miss, can I have a word, please?"

"Of course. What is it?"

"I've lost my gold ring."

"When did it go missing?"

"Last night. I always put it on my bedside cabinet, but it wasn't there when I woke up this morning."

"Could you have knocked it onto the floor by mistake?"

"I don't think so, but I didn't really have time to check."

"It's lunchtime now, so why don't you nip back to your dormitory, and take a good look around. I'll check in the staff room to see if it's been handed in."

"Thanks, Miss."

"Beth, wait. Which dorm are you in?"

"Nomad, Miss."

"Okay. I'll catch up with you there in a few minutes."

Chapter 5

The cakes had been replenished in the staff room, and it took all of my willpower to resist grabbing another one.

I checked the lost and found cupboard where any property that had been handed in was stored. Most of what was in there was rubbish: broken umbrellas, old hockey sticks and even a few old socks. On the top shelf was a small plastic box on which was scribbled the word: Valuables. It was empty except for a single necklace, which looked as though it had come out of a Christmas cracker.

"Excuse me, everyone!" I called out. "Can I have your attention for a moment?"

The room fell silent apart from Mr Humperdink who was grumbling to himself while poring over The Candle's crossword. He was as deaf as a post.

"Mr Humperdink." Mrs Daylong gave him a nudge. "Jill wants to speak to us."

"Sorry." He looked over at me. "I'm stuck on nine down."

"Beth Nightling from class one-alpha has lost her gold ring. I've just checked the lost and found cupboard, but there's nothing in there. I wondered if anyone has had it handed in to them, but not yet put it in the cupboard."

No one had.

"Did you check Fleabert Junior's pockets?" Mrs Eastwest said.

"Phil!" Mr Bluegrass, the deputy head, gave her a disapproving look. "Fleabert can be a bit of a handful, but I don't think he's a thief."

"Beth thinks it went missing in her dorm," I said. "I

doubt any of the boys would have been in there."

Miss Lombard, who, as always, was as nervous as a kitten, put her hand up, and said, "Lorraine Sharples reported that her gold ring was missing, the day before yesterday."

Mr Bluegrass came to stand by my side. "These two incidents are not necessarily related, but I suggest that we all remain vigilant. If any more items of value go missing, please report it to myself or to the headmistress."

***

The Nomad girls' dormitory was deserted except for a handful of the younger girls.

"Beth, I'm afraid the ring hasn't been handed in."

"Thanks for checking, anyway, Miss." She couldn't hide her disappointment.

"I'm sure it will turn up. One of the other teachers will let you know when it does."

"Thanks. It was a Christmas present from my grandmother. She'll be really upset when I tell her that I've lost it."

"When will you see her again?"

"Not until the end of term."

"I'm sure you'll have it back long before then, so she need never know."

Just then, a loud squawk made me jump.

"That's Rhubarb," Beth said.

"Who's Rhubarb?"

"He's a parrot, Miss."

"I didn't know you were allowed to keep pets in here."

"Only the seniors are allowed to have them. Rhubarb

belongs to Rachel Last."

The parrot squawked again.

"That must get annoying."

"You get used to it after a while."

Just then, I heard the sound of someone crying. Beth must have seen me react because she said, "It's Felicity Charming."

"Is she okay?"

"She's upset about Fluff, Miss."

"Who's Fluff?"

"I'll show you." Beth led the way down the dormitory.

At the far end of the room, sitting on her bed, was a girl with pigtails and glasses. When she noticed us, she quickly wiped her eyes and stood up.

"Are you okay?" I asked.

"Yes, Miss."

"Beth said something about *Fluff*?"

That was obviously the wrong thing to say because Felicity dissolved into tears again.

"That's Fluff over there." Beth pointed to a cage on the bedside cabinet.

"What is it?"

"No one knows." Beth shrugged.

I went over to get a closer look. The weird creature looked like a cross between a guinea pig and a miniature kangaroo, but was much fluffier than either. "He's very cute."

"Felicity found him in her backpack when she returned from a field trip to the Valley of Shadows, didn't you?"

Felicity nodded. "But they won't let me keep him, Miss. Not unless I can identify what kind of creature he is by the end of next week."

"Where's the Valley of Shadows?"

"It's about a thirty-minute walk from the school."

"I didn't think anyone was allowed outside the walls?"

"They're not usually. Only on supervised field-trips when accompanied by the protectors."

"Who are the protectors?"

"They're elite wizards that the school hires whenever there's a field trip. If a dragon was to attack, the combined power of the protectors can see them off."

"It still sounds risky."

"No one has been hurt so far, Miss."

"What exactly is the purpose of the field trips?"

"To study the flora and fauna of the surrounding area."

"I thought all of the *fauna* around these parts wanted to eat you."

"Not all of it, Miss. There are lots of harmless, small creatures like Fluff."

"And you say you found him in your bag when you got back?"

"Yes. He must have sneaked in there while we were looking at the flowers. The problem is that the school has a policy of only allowing us to keep pets under a certain size and that can be identified."

"Don't any of the teachers know what kind of creature Fluff is?"

"No, Miss. Mr Shuttlebug might have, but he died a couple of years ago."

"Was he a teacher?"

"He taught woodwork, but his hobby was the study of Candlefield's exotic creatures."

Fluff gave out a tiny squeak.

"He is cute," I said.

"Could you find out what kind of creature he is, Miss?"

"Me? I don't know the first thing about exotic animals."

"But you're a private investigator. Couldn't you investigate this for me? I could give you all of my pocket money for a month. Or two."

"I don't want your pocket money."

"Please, Miss."

"I'm not going to make promises that I can't keep. The best I can do is to ask around when I get back to Candlefield, to see if I can find anyone who knows anything about this type of creature."

"Thanks, Miss." She gave me a hug, but then realised what she'd done. "Sorry, Miss, I didn't mean—"

"That's okay. Just don't get your hopes up."

Beth and I started back down the dorm.

"What's that sorry looking object?" I pointed to the small, ugly, gold-coloured trophy on top of the bookcase.

"That's the inter-house sports cup, Miss. Nomad are the holders, and we're going to win it again this year."

"How come it's in here?"

"The winning house is allowed to keep it in their dorms. It spends alternate months in the Nomad girls' and boys' dorms."

"It's not very attractive."

"True, but it's what it represents that matters."

"Just as well."

***

I was just about to magic myself back to Washbridge when I noticed I had a text message; it was from Grandma. It must have come through while I was in the classroom when I always had my phone set to silent. She wanted me to drop in at her house to meet Madge Moleworthy.

Great! Just what I needed.

"About time." Grandma met me at the door. "I thought you were never coming."

"I didn't hear your message—"

"You're a bit young to be going deaf, aren't you?"

"I was about to say that I didn't hear it because I was at CASS."

"Doing what?"

"I teach there every other week. I did tell you."

"Oh yes, I remember now. I still can't imagine why they invited you to teach there when they could have had the benefit of my experience. My fee would have been quite reasonable."

"They wanted someone with a lot of experience of living in the human world. And, anyway, they don't pay me."

"Are you insane? Why would you do it for free?"

"Because it's a nice thing to do. It's my way of giving back. You should give it a try."

"Pah." She scoffed. "I've got better things to do with my time."

"You said in your message that you wanted me to meet Madge Moleworthy."

"She's in the kitchen."

"Hold on. What if I don't like her?"

"There's nothing not to like. Come on. My tea is going cold."

"How lovely to meet you, Jill." Madge gave me a hug. "I've heard so much about you from your grandmother. It's so kind of you to let me stay in your house while you're away."

"I haven't actually — err — think nothing of it."

"Did you want a cup of tea, Jill?" Grandma asked.

"Yes, please."

"Right. You can make us another one while you're at it. Mine's gone cold."

After I'd made the tea, we all went through to the lounge.

"Biscuit?" Grandma offered the tin to Madge and me.

"Not for me, thanks. I had a muffin at CASS."

"You've been to CASS?" Madge dunked a ginger biscuit in her tea. Gross!

"I teach there once a fortnight."

"Oh? Your grandmother told me that you were a detective."

"My main job is a private investigator in the human world. The headmistress at CASS asked if I'd teach human studies once every couple of weeks."

"Can you believe they don't even pay her?" Grandma chipped in.

"It's probably worth it just to visit CASS." Madge was trying to fish the remnants of her biscuit out of the cup of tea. "I've never been there myself, but I hear it's wonderful."

"It's a marvellous building, and the area surrounding it is —"

"Yes, yes, that's all very interesting, I'm sure." Grandma interrupted. "But Madge needs to know the arrangements for moving into your house."

"I'm planning to travel to the human world a week on Sunday," Madge said.

"Jack and I get married the day before that."

"That's alright then," Grandma said. "You can meet Madge at your house on the Sunday morning."

"I can't. We'll be on our way to our honeymoon first thing on Sunday."

"Can't you travel later?"

"No, we can't. All the arrangements have been made. Why don't I give you my key on the Saturday, Grandma, and you can let Madge have it?"

"You seem to be under the impression that I'll be coming to the wedding."

"You are, aren't you?"

"Probably. Unless I get a better offer in the meantime."

After I'd finished my tea, I made my excuses and left. I still wasn't thrilled at the idea of someone living in our house while we were away, but Madge seemed harmless enough.

Before magicking myself back to Washbridge, I nipped next door to Aunt Lucy's. Much to my surprise, the twins were both there. So too were Lil and Lil.

"Jill?" Pearl looked surprised to see me. "Come on in. I've just made tea. Would you like a cup?"

"No, thanks. I've just had a drink at Grandma's. I thought you were working today, Amber?"

"I am, but Pearl said she was going around to Mum's, so I nipped out for a few minutes. I've left Mindy in charge."

Aunt Lucy was seated on the sofa, with the two babies

on either side of her; they were both fast asleep.

"Those little angels are very peaceful," I said. "You obviously have the magical touch."

"Hmm. That's a sore point."

"What do you mean?"

"When the twins were babies, I occasionally used spells to make my life a little easier."

"What kind of spells?"

"Nothing too drastic. I used magic to rock them in their prams, or to make the cuddly toys move around. That sort of thing."

"That sounds like a great idea."

"These two don't approve." She glanced first at Pearl and then at Amber. "They've said I can't use magic around the Lils."

"I wish you wouldn't call them that," Pearl said.

"What else am I supposed to call them?"

"Lil and Lil."

"Okay." Aunt Lucy sighed. "The twins won't allow me to use magic when I'm babysitting Lil and Lil."

"Why not?" I turned to the twins. "It seems harmless enough."

"Not according to current thinking," Amber said. "All the experts say that babies should be raised without the use of magic."

Pearl nodded. "We never use magic around them at home, so we don't want Mum to do it either."

"Fair enough."

"I'd better be making tracks." Amber finished her tea, and then bent down and gave her Lil a kiss. "Bye, cutykins. Mummy will see you later."

"What time are the machine guys coming?" Pearl called

after her sister.

"In about an hour."

"Do you remember all the things you need to check with them?"

"Of course I do. Bye, everyone."

Curiosity had got the better of me, so after Amber had left, I asked Pearl who the 'machine guys' were.

"It's our latest brilliant idea for Cuppy C."

Oh no.

"I thought you'd given up on the crazy initiatives now that you have the babies."

"We still have a business to run, and anyway, this is not some crazy initiative, as you put it."

"What are you planning this time?"

"We're trying to streamline the order-taking process."

"Why do you need to do that?"

"At busy times, there can be really long queues in the tea room, even with Mindy working there."

"I haven't seen many queues."

"Yes, Jill, but you aren't there all the time like we are, are you?"

"True. Why don't you just employ more assistants?"

"There isn't room behind the counter. That's why we came up with the idea of using machines to take the orders."

"What kind of machines? You aren't thinking of using robots, are you?"

"Of course not. We're not stupid. They'd be bound to go wrong. We're going to get those self-order machines you sometimes see in fast-food restaurants."

"I know the sort of thing you mean. They're very

complicated. It took me ages to work out how to use them."

"They're not complicated." She laughed. "Well, for you, maybe, but most people find them easy to use. And they're really quick. You place your order, and by the time you get to the counter, it's waiting for you to collect."

"Aren't they expensive?"

"That's what we thought until Ron came to see us."

"Ron?"

"Yeah. Ron Gunn. He supplies reconditioned machines for a fraction of the cost of new. We'll only need a couple of them, so they'll pay for themselves in no time."

"Reconditioned? Isn't that a bit dodgy?"

"Not at all. They're fully guaranteed."

"What do you think about this, Aunt Lucy?"

"There's no point in asking me, Jill. We oldies don't know anything, apparently."

***

I spent the afternoon in the office, but there was nothing much doing—not so much as a sniff of a new client. I was beginning to think that Winky's suggestion that I move into the Feng Shui business was worth more consideration. How difficult could it be to shuffle furniture around a room? The hard part would be keeping a straight face while talking earnestly about the negative and positive energy flows. But let's face it, you'd have to be pretty unscrupulous to do something like that.

What do you mean it should suit me down to the ground?

The afternoon really dragged, and even when it was finally time to call it a day, I still had to face the tedious dress fitting.

I was just wondering whether or not anyone would notice if I didn't turn up when Kathy and Lizzie walked into my office.

"Didn't you trust me to come to the shop?" I said.

"Lizzie has something she wants to ask you, don't you, Pumpkin?"

"Auntie Jill, can I borrow your cat?"

"Winky? What do you want him for?"

"Cheryl and Amy—they're my friends at school. They've both entered their cats in the cat show, and I'd like to enter Winky."

"Couldn't you just go and watch it?"

"That wouldn't be as much fun. Mummy said you might let me enter Winky into the competition."

"I'm not sure he'd enjoy being in a cat show." Just then, I spotted Winky who had come out from under the sofa. He was giving me two thumbs up and nodding his head. "Then again, I suppose he might like it."

"Thank you, Auntie Jill." She threw her arms around me. "You're the best auntie in the whole wide world."

"That's okay. When is it?"

"This Sunday." Kathy held up three tickets.

"*This* Sunday? The day after the hen night?"

"You did say you wouldn't be having much to drink."

"I know, but—hold on a minute. How come you already have the tickets?"

"They were selling out fast. I had to make sure they didn't run out." She fished another piece of paper out of her pocket. "And this is confirmation that Winky has been entered into the competition."

"I can't wait," Lizzie gushed.

"Me neither." I glared at Kathy.

"We'd better get back to the shop." Kathy took Lizzie's hand. "We'll see you down there in a few minutes, Auntie Jill." She was almost out of the door when she said, "Oh, and don't worry about the money for the tickets and the entrance fee. You can give it to me later."

Once again, that sister of mine had done me up like a kipper.

"What do I win?" Winky jumped onto my desk.

"What?"

"At the cat show. I'm bound to win. What's the prize?"

"How would I know? Are you really sure you want to do this? There's still time to back out."

"No chance. I'm really looking forward to it."

***

"I'll get you back for this," I said when I arrived at the bridal shop.

"For what?" Kathy gave me an innocent look.

"You know what. The cat show."

"It'll be fun, just you, me and Lizzie."

"Says you. Do we really need to bother with another dress fitting tonight? It was perfect the last time I tried it on."

"No, it wasn't. The hem on one side at the back was half a centimetre too long."

"I want to see your dress again, Auntie Jill." Lizzie was already wearing her bridesmaid's dress.

"You look beautiful, Lizzie." I glanced around. "Where's Mikey?"

"There's something I have to tell you about Mikey," Kathy said.

"He's not poorly, is he?"

"No, he's fine, but he's decided he doesn't want to be a pageboy."

"Why?"

"Apparently, some of his friends saw a photo of him, and made fun of his outfit."

"He shouldn't care what they say."

"That's what I told him, but he's adamant he doesn't want to do it. I even tried to bribe him with the promise of maggots."

"*Maggots*?"

"For his fishing. He's always running out of them, but even the promise of a month's supply wasn't enough to change his mind."

"It's okay. I wouldn't expect him to do it unless he wants to. I'm happy just to have you and Lizzie as bridesmaids."

"Come on, then. Put the dress on. Let me take a look at that hem."

***

As Jack was having a bowling night, I called at the fish and chip shop on my way home from the dress fitting. Tish and Chip were behind the counter.

"Fish, chips and mushy peas, please."

"Open or wrapped?"

"Wrapped, please."

"Salt and vinegar?"

"No, thanks."

"What about curtains?"

"Sorry?"

"We have a promotion on ready-made curtains this week." She pointed to the display at the far end of the counter.

"Err—no, thanks. I'm good for curtains."

Despite their inexplicable obsession with soft furnishings, Tish and Chip did make delicious fish and chips. I ate every last morsel.

Jack arrived home just before ten-thirty. "It smells of fish and chips in here."

"I called at the chippy on my way home."

"Too lazy to make yourself something?"

"No. I had to go for the dress fitting after work, and I didn't get away from there for ages. You know what Kathy's like—fussing around."

"How did it go?"

"Okay. Apparently, the hem is spot on now."

"Good stuff."

"Mikey isn't going to be our pageboy."

"Oh? Why not?"

"His friends were taking the mickey, so he's decided he doesn't want to do it."

"How do you feel about that?"

"Fine. It's best he doesn't do it if he doesn't want to. He'd only act up on the day. How did the bowling go?"

"Brilliant. I told you that Bill and Graham had challenged me and Chris to the best of five matches, didn't I?"

"Err—yeah, I think so." I normally zoned out when Jack was talking about bowling.

"Well, we beat them tonight."

"That's nice."

"*Nice*? It's unbelievable. Nibbler is favourite for next month's North of England Cup; he's won three years in a row. And—"

"Hold on. Did you call him Nibbler?"

"That's Bill's nickname because he bites his nails non-stop."

"You should introduce him to Deli's husband. It sounds like they'd hit it off. So, what's your nickname?"

"I don't have one. Anyway, I was telling you about our fantastic victory. Graham is second seed for the North of England Cup. When Bill and Graham play as a team, they're practically invincible. In fact, that's what they'd taken to calling themselves: the invincibles. They even have matching shirts and bowling balls."

"Well done you."

"Thanks. It felt good to get the better of them after all this time."

"Should I start to call you King Pin?"

"I think you should."

Chapter 6

The next morning, Jack was still basking in the glory of his bowling victory. I tried to be enthusiastic, but I was only half awake and much more interested in the full English he'd made for both of us.

"I've been thinking," I said, during a break in the frame by frame analysis of the previous night's match. "I think we should get the sandpit taken out."

"What brought that up?"

"It's just that every morning when I come into the kitchen, I see it through the window, and wonder why we've got it."

"You were the one who wanted it in the first place."

"I know, but Mikey's never been bothered about it, and even Lizzie seems to have grown tired of it. She didn't go anywhere near it the last two times she came over. I thought it might be nice to reclaim our garden."

"Can we afford it, what with all the wedding expenses?"

"Have you forgotten my brother-in-law is in the landscaping business? I'm sure Peter would be happy to do it for free."

"You can't expect him to do that. He's running a business."

"I was only joking about him doing it for free, but I bet he'll give us a really good deal."

"What about those funny little creatures that used to live in there?"

"Joey and Zoe? They moved out months ago, which is another good reason to get rid of it before some other sand sloths claim it for their home. I'll have a word with

Kathy and get her to mention it to Peter."

Jack is a really slow eater. I'd already cleared my plate by the time he was half-way through his.

"Hey!" He knocked away my fork with his. "Leave my sausages alone."

"I didn't think you were going to eat them both."

"Why would you think that?"

"You have the look of a man who is going to leave a sausage uneaten."

"I'll have you know that I intend to eat all of my sausages, and all of my bacon, and everything else on my plate, but I'd enjoy it a whole lot more if I didn't have you hovering over me like a vulture."

"Charming." I stood up from the table. "I know when I'm not wanted."

My husband-to-be could be so selfish sometimes.

I had to get out of the kitchen, otherwise I would have succumbed to the urge to grab one of his sausages, with or without his permission.

"Hey, Jack, it looks like our new next-door neighbour has moved in," I shouted from the lounge.

"I don't believe you. That's just a ruse to get me to leave my breakfast unattended."

"It's true, there's a van parked on the driveway. You should go around there and say hello."

"And leave my breakfast for you to eat? No chance."

Drat. He'd seen right through my cunning plan.

Just then, Jack's phone rang.

"Chris? Good morning, Buddy."

Chris Jardine was Jack's bowling partner. He'd no

doubt called Jack, so they could revel some more in their victory. I figured the phone call might have distracted him from his breakfast, so made my way furtively back through to the kitchen.

"What? How?"

I could tell from Jack's voice and expression that something was badly wrong.

"I can't believe it. How did you hear? Right. Okay, thanks for calling."

"What's wrong?" I asked as soon as he was off the call.

"It's Bill Mellor. He died last night. Chris just got a call from Bill's wife. Apparently, he collapsed not long after he got in from bowling."

"That's terrible. I'm so sorry."

Jack stood up and walked over to the window. "He was fine last night when we said our goodbyes."

"Do they know what it was?"

"Chris didn't say. A heart attack, I assume. Poor Crystal."

"I take it Crystal is Bill's wife?"

"Yes, she must be devastated." Jack gestured to his breakfast. "You can have what's left of that if you want. I'm going to get ready for work."

Needless to say, my appetite had vanished.

Understandably, Jack was still very subdued when he set off for work.

"Be careful." He gave me a kiss. "Don't take any unnecessary risks."

"I won't. I promise. See you tonight."

I left for work fifteen minutes later, and I'd no sooner walked out of the door when a familiar, but unwelcome, voice called my name.

"Morning, Jill!"

"Mr Ivers?"

He was standing on next door's driveway.

"Beautiful morning, isn't it?"

"What are you doing here? Are you delivering something?"

"No, I live here. We're neighbours."

"*You've* moved in next door?" The full horror of the situation hit home.

"Yes, I bought it with some of the money from my lottery win. Are you feeling alright, Jill? You're looking a little pale."

"I'm okay. Someone told me about your lottery win. Are you renting this place? I assume it's just a stopgap until you find somewhere else?"

"No, I bought it outright. I plan to be here for a long, long time. Probably the rest of my life."

"That's—err—great. Just great. What about your job? I heard you'd given up working at the toll bridge."

"And thank goodness for that. My elbows were in a terrible state. I've started my own business now." He pointed to the van.

"Have Ivers Got A Movie For You?"

"Catchy name, don't you think?"

"I guess so. What kind of business is it, exactly?"

"Movie rental—door-to-door."

"I'm no expert but haven't you missed the boat a little there?"

"I know what you're thinking. Silly Ivers has landed himself with a load of VHS movies that nobody wants anymore. Fear not. I'm on the cutting edge of the industry.

All my movies are on DVD."

"Right. Don't you think streaming has taken over the market?"

"*Streaming*? What's that?"

"Never mind. I'm sure it'll be a great success."

"Your luck is in because I'm offering a special discount for the first one hundred customers."

"How many have you signed up?"

"None yet. I only took delivery of the van and the DVDs last Friday. Today is day one. What do you say, would you like to be my first customer?"

"Thanks for the generous offer, but Jack and I never watch movies."

"Really?" He looked horrified. "What do you watch?"

"Jack mainly watches TenPin TV, and I prefer educational documentaries." I made a show of checking my watch. "Is that the time? I'd better get going. Bye, Mr Ivers."

"Bye, neighbour."

I must have done something really awful in a previous life to have deserved this. Just when I thought I'd seen the last of Ivers, he turns up as my new neighbour. Again.

***

"Morning, Jill."

I still hadn't got used to seeing Mrs V's desk on the opposite side of the room.

"Morning, Mrs V. I see the tripwire has gone."

"They came to do it first thing this morning. A nice young man with a green beard."

"Green?"

"I think he must have dyed it."

"I certainly hope so."

"He made short work of putting in a new socket. I gave him a scarf and a pair of socks. Green to match his beard."

"Nice."

"Have you thought anymore about having Brian work his magic on your office?"

"I don't think I'm going to bother."

"I know it seems expensive, but it would soon pay for itself with the increased productivity."

"Even so. I like things the way they are."

"You know best, dear. How did the dress fitting go last night?"

"Okay. The hem is apparently now perfection itself."

"How did the little ones look?"

"Lizzie's dress is gorgeous, but it seems we aren't going to have a pageboy. Mikey has said he doesn't want to do it."

"Is Kathy going to try to change his mind?"

"It would be a waste of time, and besides, I wouldn't want him to do it unless he wanted to." I started towards my office door, but then remembered something I'd been meaning to do. "Mrs V, would you contact Sid Song at 'It's A Sign' and ask him if he can make a new sign for me?"

"What's wrong with the one you've got?"

"I'll be taking Jack's name, so I want the new sign to reflect that."

"I assumed you'd keep the business under the old name."

"It would get too confusing; I'd rather just have a clean

break. Tell Sid that if he can do the new sign for the same price as the old one, you can give him the go-ahead, but if he wants more money, tell him you'll shop around."

"Will do."

"Ideally, I'd like it to be installed while I'm away on honeymoon."

"I'll tell him that."

"Oh, and I should warn you. Sid is a strange kind of a guy. He doesn't so much speak as sing."

"That's okay, dear. I'm used to working with strange people."

Burn.

"I'm going to need some cash," Winky said as soon as I walked into my office.

"For what?"

"To hire a tux, and I'll need a new shirt and tie."

"What are you talking about?"

"My outfit for the wedding. I heard you tell the old bag lady that your nephew has left you in the lurch."

Oh bum! Me and my big mouth.

"I don't think we're going to bother with a pageboy. Or cat. I think we'll just stick with the bridesmaids."

"You promised. You gave me your solemn word that if Mickey—"

"Mikey."

"Whatever. You said that if he dropped out, I could step in for him."

"Yeah, but things have changed."

"How?"

"When I said that, I didn't think there was any possibility that it would ever happen."

Winky turned his back on me. "I've had my heart set on this." He snuffled, and for a moment, I thought he was about to cry. "I really thought you meant it this time."

"Winky."

"It's alright. I'm sure I'll get over it. Eventually."

"Maybe, err—"

He turned around. "Yes?"

"Well, I suppose—"

"Yes?"

"You'd have to do exactly what I say."

"Of course. I'm at your command."

What had I just done?

***

Later that morning, I was still trying to work out how to tell Jack that we would have a pagecat at our wedding, when Mrs V came through to my office.

"Jill, there's a strange little man out there."

"Strange how?"

"Just strange."

"Did he say what he wanted?"

"Just that he may have information that will be useful to you."

"What's his name?"

"I'm not sure. I asked a couple of times, but I couldn't make out what he said."

"Okay. You'd better show him in."

The man, who was short and quite skinny, walked with a stoop.

"Good morning, Mr—"

"Manic."

"Mr *Manic*?"

"It's just Manic."

"Right. Would you care to take a seat?"

"Manic prefers to stand."

"Okay." Here's a golden rule to live your life by: Stay far away from anyone who refers to themselves in the third person. "How can I help you, err — Manic?"

"You can't."

"Right, so what's the purpose of your visit today?"

"Manic can help you."

"And how exactly can you do that?"

"Manic knows people."

If I'd had a panic alarm installed, now would have been the time to press it.

"I'm not sure what you're getting at."

"You're a private investigator. Right?"

"That's right."

"Exactly."

Oh boy.

"Look, I'm sorry, but I don't have the first idea what you're talking about."

"Manic knows a lot of people — bad people. Manic hears things — interesting things. Manic gives stories to the press and gets paid for them."

"Right."

"Manic can help you, too."

"How exactly?"

"When you need information, you come to Manic. He finds the information you need. Then you pay Manic. Everyone is happy."

"To be perfectly honest, I can't imagine ever needing

your — err — services."

"Others have told Manic the same thing, but they're usually wrong." He dug into his pocket and dropped a grubby business card onto my desk. The only thing printed on it was a phone number. "Call this number and leave a message. Manic will call you back."

"Right, but like I said — "

He stood up. "Manic will see himself out."

"Who was that weirdo?" Winky came out from under the sofa.

"I've no idea, but I feel like I need a shower."

"Anyway, about the cash for the tux."

Before I could respond, my phone rang; it was Jack.

"Jill, I've just had a call from one of my old oppos at Washbridge police station. He wasn't supposed to tell me, but he knew that Bill Mellor was a friend of mine."

"Tell you what?"

"It seems that Bill didn't die from natural causes. They say he was poisoned."

"Accidentally?"

"I don't know. They want the three of us: me, Chris and Graham to call in so they can interview us. I've said I'll go in this afternoon, so it's just possible that I'll be late home tonight."

"Could it be something he ate at the bowling alley last night? What about you? Are you feeling okay?"

"I'm fine. We didn't really have much to eat — just a burger and a coke."

"Okay. Keep me posted."

"Will do. See you tonight."

Winky cleared his throat to get my attention. He was holding out his paw.

"How much is this tux going to cost me?" I said.

"A hundred should do it."

"You don't need to buy one. You can just hire it."

"That is the cost to hire it. Feline tuxes aren't ten a penny, you know."

I checked my purse. "I've only got seventy-five pounds."

"That'll do." He snatched the cash from my hand. "You won't regret it. I'll be the smartest pagecat you've ever seen."

And the first.

Winky disappeared out of the window just as Mrs V came through to my office.

"What did that creepy little man want?"

"I honestly don't have any idea. I think he was a lettuce short of a sandwich."

"Shouldn't that be a sandwich short of a picnic?"

"Lettuce, sandwich? Same difference."

"I've been thinking about your pageboy situation, Jill, and maybe I can help."

"How do you mean?"

"Do you remember the pageboy issue I had at my wedding?"

"Andy and Randy?"

"Andy and Raymond, actually, but yes. If you recall, I was worried about having both of them as pageboys in case they started fighting."

"I never did find out how you resolved that situation. From what I remember, they both behaved perfectly on the day. How did you manage that?"

"I drugged them."

"What?"

"I'm only joking. I bribed them both. I said I'd give them cash if they got through the ceremony without any problems, and they did. Anyway, I was thinking that maybe you could 'borrow' one of my pageboys for your big day. Andy or Raymond, you could have your pick."

"That's very thoughtful, Mrs V, but I've managed to sort out the pageboy problem. We're going to have — err — that's to say — err — we've decided not to bother."

"Are you sure?"

"Positive, but thanks for the offer."

Chapter 7

Winky had taken the last of my cash for his tux, so I had to nip out to the ATM. When I checked the balance, I was pleasantly surprised to see there was a little more in the account than I'd expected. Jack and I had separate personal bank accounts plus a joint one used for all the household bills. He was much more sensible with money than I was, and no doubt had a bazillion pounds in his account. Even though I always worked to a really tight budget, I was lucky if my balance was still in double figures by the end of each month.

What do you mean, I should cut down on the muffins and custard creams? Everyone deserves a little treat occasionally. It's not like I overindulge.

While I was out of the office, I decided to call in at Coffee Games for a coffee and a—err—nothing. Just a coffee. No muffins would pass my lips. Definitely not.

"Daze? How come you're in here? Where's Blaze?"

"He's ill. He had to go home yesterday."

"Oh dear. Nothing serious, I hope?"

"It turns out he's allergic to dominoes."

I laughed.

"I'm not joking. Apparently, it's a little-known allergy called Dominitus. He was covered in little red blotches."

"Poor thing. I hope he's okay."

"He'll be fine. What can I get for you?"

"I'll have a caramel latte, please."

"Is that all?" She gave me a puzzled look. "Why are you making hand signals, Jill?"

"Shush! You never know who might be listening."

"Are you pointing to the muffins?"

Drat. So much for my attempt at subterfuge.

"Would you like a board game to go with that? It's Cluedo today."

"Not for me, thanks. I can't stay long."

The shop was very busy, so I was forced to take the table next to the door—not one of my favourites because there was a draught every time someone went in or out.

I'd just taken a sip of coffee when the man on the next table got down on his hands and knees and crawled under my table.

"Excuse me. What are you doing?"

"Sorry." He popped his head up. "I've lost my lead piping. You haven't seen it, have you?"

"No. Have you tried the conservatory?"

What? Come on. That was not only comedy genius but lightning quick too.

"Very amusing." He grimaced. "Ah, here it is." He held up the tiny piece. "Aren't you playing Cluedo?"

"No, I'm here by myself."

"You should come and join in with our game. We've only just started. I'm Bob Green. I'm here with my girlfriend, Scarlet."

"Green and Scarlet." I laughed. "That's very funny."

"Sorry?"

"They're both characters from Cluedo."

"Are they? Oh yes, so they are. It had never occurred to me."

Wow! Just wow!

"Why don't you come and join our game?"

"Thanks for the offer, but I have to go soon."

I'd finished my drink and was about to leave when in

walked Blaze.

"Hi, Jill. I see you've just polished off another muffin."

"Err—no. That must be someone else's plate. I only had a coffee."

"Of course you did." He grinned.

"I'm glad to see you've recovered from the Dominitus."

"The what?"

"Your allergy to dominoes. Daze told me all about it." I glanced over at the counter to see her bent double with laughter. "You're not allergic to them at all, are you?"

"Err—no. Is anyone? Daze was covering for me while I went to the dentist."

***

I'd no sooner left Coffee Games than Betty Longbottom came rushing across the road to me.

"Jill, you haven't forgotten about the big event, have you?"

"I know I can be forgetful at times, Betty, but I'm hardly likely to forget my own wedding, am I?"

"I'm talking about the grand opening of The Sea's The Limit. It's this Friday. You have to come."

"It's finally ready, then?"

"Yes, thank goodness. We've had so many delays and setbacks that I was beginning to think this day would never arrive. We still haven't received the licence to allow us to keep the dangerous species yet, but hopefully that won't be much longer. You will come, won't you?"

"Yeah, sure."

"Bring both of your PAs, too."

"I only have the one now. Jules left to go and work at

Washbridge police station. I'm sure Mrs V will come though."

"Great. It starts at ten o'clock. Don't be late because there's likely to be a big crowd."

"Okay. See you then."

Betty skipped back across the road, full of the joys of Spring.

"Did I hear you correctly, Gooder? You're getting married?"

I turned around to find Ma Chivers standing behind me. I hadn't seen her for over a year—the last time had been shortly after Grandma's moles had undermined Yarnstormers and caused it to collapse.

"Hello, Ma. I thought you'd crawled back into your hole and decided to stay there."

"I've been on a sabbatical, but it seems I came back just in time."

"For what?"

"Your wedding of course. I assume my invitation is in the post?"

"I wouldn't hold your breath."

"It would be a shame if anything happened to spoil your big day."

"Is that a threat?"

"Of course not. I'm just saying that it would be terrible if something awful happened."

"You don't scare me, Ma."

"That's exactly what Alicia said."

"Where is Alicia, anyway? I haven't seen her for ages. What did you do to her?"

"Me? Nothing. You know me—I wouldn't harm a flea.

Anyway, nice speaking to you as always, Gooder. My regards to Jack."

It took all of my willpower not to use a lightning bolt on her, there and then. Where was Alicia? It was over a year since I'd seen her too, and I had a horrible feeling she might have met a sticky end.

I was still seething about Ma Chivers when my phone rang.

"Jill, it's Desdemona Nightowl."

"Is everything okay?"

"I'm afraid not. We have a bit of a problem, and I'm hoping you might be able to help. Do you think you could pop over to my office straight away?"

"Of course. I'll be with you in a couple of minutes."

I magicked myself to the west wing of CASS, and from there made my way to the headmistress' office.

"Come in, Jill. Thanks for coming over so quickly. I know how busy you must be. Please, take a seat. Would you like a drink?"

"No, thanks. I've just had a coffee. No muffins, though—in case you were wondering."

"Right."

"It's ages since I had one. A muffin, that is."

"Okay, I'm glad we've cleared that up. As I said on the phone, we have something of a tricky problem. As you know, it's the inter-house sports competition a week on Friday. Unfortunately, the cup has gone missing."

"Really? I only saw it yesterday when I was in the Nomad girls' dorm with Beth Nightling."

"It disappeared overnight."

"Do you have any visitors here at CASS at the

moment?"

"None, which I'm afraid must mean it was taken by one of the pupils or a member of staff."

"I can't imagine why anyone would want to steal it. It's rather ugly."

"Granted, it isn't the prettiest trophy in the world, but it is quite valuable."

"Really?"

"You realise it's made of real gold?"

"I never would have guessed, but then it looked in dire need of a clean when I saw it."

"That's the problem with allowing the winning house to keep it in their dorms. There are so many grubby hands on it."

"I'm surprised you allow them to keep something of such value on open display in there."

"It's a school tradition which dates back to the start of the inter-house sports competition. This is the first time we've had a problem."

"I assume you have no idea who might be responsible."

"None, but the accusations have already started to fly."

"Oh?"

"A number of people have pointed the finger at Toyah Harlow, the Nomad house captain."

"What makes them think she might have stolen it?"

"There's been some suggestion that she's hidden the trophy because she fears Nomad will lose out in next week's competition. That's complete nonsense, in my opinion, and I've warned the children that if I hear anyone make any more unsubstantiated accusations, they'll have me to answer to. The whole thing has left a dark cloud over the school and has put next week's competition in doubt. That's why I called you."

"It might be best if I start by speaking to all of the house captains together."

"I agree, but as important as this issue is, the children are all sitting midterm exams today. I couldn't justify pulling them out of those. What about tomorrow?"

"That'll be fine."

"Excellent. I'll call you later to arrange a time."

"While I'm here, Headmistress, can I ask you about Mr Shuttlebug?"

"Cuthbert? Such a terrible loss. What did you want to know, exactly?"

"I believe he had an interest in the exotic creatures of these regions."

"An interest?" She smiled. "An obsession, more like. He spent every spare minute on that book of his."

"He wrote a book?"

"It was his life's work. Unfortunately, it was never published. He couldn't get a publisher interested, which is a tragedy when you consider some of the rubbish they publish these days."

"Do you know what happened to the book?"

"I imagine his widow will have it. Poor Deloris. She took Cuthbert's death very hard, as you might imagine."

"I'm sure. You don't happen to have her address, do you?"

***

Midway through the afternoon, I got a call from Jack to say he was on his way to my office. I asked why, but he said he was only two minutes away, and that he'd explain when he arrived.

"What do you think?" Winky swaggered up the office in his tux.

"You have to hide. Get under the sofa."

"Why?"

"Jack's on his way over. He can't see you dressed like that."

"Why not? He's going to see me at the wedding."

"I—err—I want it to be a surprise for him on the day."

"That makes sense, but I can't go under the sofa. It's dusty under there."

"Okay. Get in here." I opened the cupboard door.

"I can't go in there either. I'm claustrophobic."

"It'll only be for a few minutes. Go on." I gave him a gentle nudge.

Okay, so it wasn't all that gentle.

"It's dark in here."

"Shush!"

Just then, Jack arrived.

"What's wrong?" I said.

"I can't believe it. Chris Jardine has been charged with Bill's murder."

"What?"

"It's insane. Chris wouldn't hurt a fly."

"You said Bill had been poisoned, didn't you?"

"Yes. I assumed it was food poisoning, but it sounds like the poison was on his fingers when he bit his fingernails."

"How do you know all of this?"

"One of my old buddies at Washbridge police station gave me a call. He'll be in a whole heap of trouble if anyone finds out that he's contacted me. As far as I can make out, they charged Chris because they found traces of the poison on a cigarette butt that Bill had dropped."

"How does that tie into Chris?"

"Bill was supposed to have given up smoking, so he never had any cigarettes of his own. He was always bumming them off Chris. When I left them last night, they were having a crafty smoke."

"Is there any possibility at all that Chris could have murdered Bill?"

"None. I've never been more certain of anything in my life. The trouble is I can't do anything to help him. If I get involved, I'll be thrown out of the force because I'm a friend of the suspect, and anyway, this is no longer my patch. That's why I came to see you."

"You want me to investigate?"

"Yes, but you'll have to be discreet."

"I always am."

"Your idea of discreet and mine are very different, but this time, you'll have to be ultra-careful not to tread on any toes—particularly not Sue Shay's. If it gets out that you're doing this for me, I'll be for the high jump."

"Don't worry. You can trust me."

"Thanks. It's not worth my going back to West Chipping now, so I reckon I'll head home."

"Yeah, me too. I need to call in at the shop on my way in, so I'll see you at the house."

We kissed, and then he left. I was just about to follow when I heard a muffled voice.

"Let me out!"

"Sorry, Winky, I'd forgotten you were in there."

"I was almost out of air." He stumbled out.

"Don't be so melodramatic. There are plenty of holes in that old cupboard."

***

My visit to the corner shop was to pick up essential supplies.

"Anything apart from the custard creams, Jill?" Little Jack Corner had taken to wearing bow ties; today's little number was orange.

"No, thanks. Just those."

"One, two, three, four packets. Will that be enough?"

"Yes, they should keep me going for quite some time."

"Like the four packets you bought two days ago?"

"I'm sure it was much longer ago than that."

"It's definitely two days. I remember because I was wearing my favourite bow tie—the purple one."

"We've had quite a few visitors to the house since then," I lied. "They ate most of the biscuits." I glanced around. "I haven't seen Missy for a while."

"Didn't you know? She handed in her notice and left a month ago."

"I thought she liked working here?"

"She did, but then out of the blue, she quit."

"Do you know why?"

"Yes, and it was for a really silly reason. She was in the store room, eating her lunch when a giant spider came down from the ceiling and sat next to her. It scared her to death. I tried to talk her into staying, but she'd made her mind up that she wanted out. Last I heard, she was working as an admin assistant in a solicitor's office: Birds and Day, I think."

"That must have left you shorthanded?"

"It did for a while, but I've managed to recruit a replacement." He took out his walkie-talkie. "Lucy? Lucy, are you there? Over?" There was no reply, so he tried again, but without any luck. "Where is that girl?" He came out from behind the counter and started down one of the aisles.

I followed.

Standing next to the freezers, was a young woman with curly, ginger hair. She was wearing huge gloves.

"Lucy. Why didn't you pick up when I called?" Little Jack Corner said.

"Sorry, Jack." She held up her hands. "The walkie-talkie is in my pocket, and I couldn't get it out with these gloves on."

"Never mind. This is the customer I told you about. The one who buys ninety percent of our custard creams."

"I'm sure it isn't that many." I laughed. "I'm pleased to meet you. I'm Jill."

"Nice to meet you too, Jill. I'm Lucy. Lucy Locket."

Chapter 8

The next morning when I came downstairs, Jack was on his phone.

"Just a minute, Sarah. Jill's here now. It's Sarah — Chris's wife. Will you be able to go and see her this morning?"

"Of course. What time?"

"Sarah, what time would be good for you? Nine-thirty?"

I nodded.

"That's fine. Jill will see you then. Try to keep your chin up. Everything's going to be okay."

"How did she sound?" I asked when he'd ended the call.

"Not great. She's worried sick. Chris hasn't been in the best of health recently, so there's no telling what this kind of stress might do to him. Will you let me know how you get on?"

"Sure."

"Have you seen our new next-door neighbour yet?" Jack asked after he'd finished his breakfast.

"I have, unfortunately. It's Mr Ivers."

"Why do I recognise that name?"

"He was one of my neighbours at my old place, and he worked in the pay-booth at the toll-bridge until recently."

"The weird little guy with the mechanical arm."

"Andy."

"Is that his name?"

"No, that was the name of his mechanical arm. I can't remember Ivers' first name — oh, hang on. It's Montgomery, I think. I can't believe he's moved in next door. That man has been the bane of my life for years now."

"Is he married?"

"No. I seem to remember a couple of girlfriends, but they didn't last long. Hardly surprising because he could bore for England."

"Is he working for himself now? I saw his van but couldn't make head or tail of the name."

"He's in the door-to-door movie rental business, apparently. I give it six months."

"He must be doing okay if he can afford to buy next door."

"He paid for that with his lottery win."

"He won the lottery?"

"Not the jackpot, but enough to buy the house and set up his new business. He's hoping to make a living renting out movies on DVD. And get this: he's never heard of movie streaming."

"Oh dear."

"You said it. And while we're on the subject of Mr Ivers, whatever you do, don't get too friendly with him. Under no circumstances, must you ever invite him over here. I won't be responsible for my actions if you do."

"He can't be that bad."

"Trust me, he's worse. Much worse."

Jack had finished his breakfast and gone through to the lounge to get his morning update from TenPin TV. I was still chewing my way through a bowl of muesli, which in a moment of madness, I'd allowed Jack to persuade me to have for breakfast.

How did he eat this stuff?

"Jill! Come and look at this!"

"Okay." Any excuse to get away from the muesli.

"Look." He pointed out of the window. "I haven't seen that thing for ages."

Neither had I, and I'd hoped never to see it again. Parked at the bottom of our drive was Bessie, Mr Hosey's ridiculous train. The last time I'd seen that stupid thing, it had been lying on its side, having crashed into another train owned by Mr Kilbride, our kilt-making ex-neighbour.

Mr Hosey jumped out of the engine and looked our way.

"Duck!" I stooped down below the level of the window. "Don't let him see us."

"Too late." Jack laughed. "He's coming up the drive."

"Don't answer the door. He'll think we've gone to work."

"Both of our cars are on the drive."

"Maybe he'll think we're having a lie in."

"He's already seen me."

"Why didn't you hide?"

"Err—because I'm not insane? Come on. Let's see what he wants."

"Whatever you do, don't let him in this house." I followed Jack to the door.

"Morning, Jack," Mr Hosey said. "Where's Jill—oh, there you are. I almost didn't see you behind the door."

"Morning, Mr Hosey," Jack said. "I see you've got your train back on the road."

"Indeed, but only after much blood, sweat and tears. It cost a small fortune to repair, but it was worth every penny, wouldn't you say?"

"It's looking very good." Jack nodded.

I managed a grunt.

"A little bird tells me that you two are tying the knot next week."

Oh no. Hosey must have come around to angle for an invite. I had to act quickly before Jack said something I'd regret.

"Whoops, sorry." I nudged Jack to one side. "I'm afraid we weren't able to invite you, Mr Hosey. It's going to be a very small affair. Relatives and close family friends only. Isn't that right, Jack?"

"Err — yeah."

"That's okay," Mr Hosey said. "I wasn't expecting an invitation."

Phew.

"We'd better get a move on." I started to close the door. "We both have work today."

"Just a moment, Jill. I haven't told you my reason for calling yet. As you might imagine, repairing Bessie has been very expensive. I was forced to take out a small bank loan, which I'm keen to pay off as soon as possible."

"We really don't need any more of your Bessie T-shirts."

"Just as well because I've sold out of them. Actually, I've come to the realisation that if I'm to keep Bessie on the road, she'll have to pay for her own upkeep. With that in mind, I racked my brain to think of a way to do that. And I'm pleased to report that I have come up with what I'm sure you'll agree is a brilliant plan. Would you like to know what it is?"

Before I could say 'no', he continued.

"Weddings!"

"Sorry?"

"These days, it's become rather old hat for the bride to travel in a limousine, wouldn't you say?"

"I — err —"

"You must have noticed the increased use of horse and carriage, for example."

"I've seen a few, but I —"

"So, I thought to myself: What if the bride was to travel to the wedding by train?"

"On Bessie?"

"Exactly."

"I'm not sure anyone would want —"

"I expect people to be queuing around the block once I've launched the service formally."

"I'm really not convinced that —"

"Fortunately, I'm in a position to offer you the service for free. A kind of soft launch which I can use as a reference."

"Me? Travel to my wedding on that —"

"That's a very kind offer," Jack cut me off. "The thing is, Mr Hosey, we already have the limousines booked, and we can't cancel so close to the big day. We'd lose all of our money."

"That's very disappointing." Mr Hosey looked crestfallen. "Are you sure I can't change your mind?"

"No, I'm sorry." Jack ushered me inside. "Thanks anyway for the offer."

"That man is certifiable," I said, once Hosey had driven away in Bessie. "Who in their right mind would travel to their wedding on a toy train?"

"You can't fault him for effort."

"Speaking of the wedding, what are your thoughts on animals?"

"Sorry?"

"When I was at the dress fitting, I was so bored that I looked through a few bridal magazines. There were several photographs of couples who had included their pets in the wedding ceremony."

"Dogs?"

"Yeah, mainly."

"I think it's rather sad to dress dogs in silly outfits."

"I thought they looked kind of cute."

"I don't think so. Anyway, what does it matter? It's not like we have a dog. By the way, have you let your mum and dad know about the seating arrangements yet?"

"Not yet, no."

"You better had. I know they were hoping to be nearer to the action, but it's really not going to be possible."

"I'll tell them today."

***

Sarah Jardine lived in a semi-detached house that was only a stone's throw from my old flat. I was running a little early, so I called into what had once been my local newsagent's. Behind the counter was Jasper James, who still favoured the fedora — today's was a rather fetching cream colour.

"Morning, Jasper."

"Well, I never. Hello, young lady. What brings you back to these parts?"

"I'm here to interview someone, but I need a snack first because I didn't get much breakfast this morning." I grabbed a KitKat from the display.

"Would you like a magazine while you're here?"

"No, thanks. I don't get much time to read these days."

"That isn't a problem. I've recently started to sell audio magazines, and I think I have just the one for you."

"Thanks, but I really don't—"

"Muffin Monthly. There's a special feature this month on blueberry muffins."

"Really? That does sound quite interesting. How exactly do the audio magazines work?"

"All I need is your phone number; the magazine will automatically be sent to your phone."

"Are they expensive?"

"Not at all. Only five-ninety-nine."

"Go on, then." I gave him my number and then paid by card.

I still had a few minutes before my meeting with Sarah Jardine, so I listened to the audio magazine which had already appeared on my phone.

As reported in last month's issue of Muffin Monthly, sales of blueberry muffins in the UK have increased dramatically over the last two years. If sales of blueberry remain at this level, we may see their sales overtake those of chocolate chip for the first time. Industry leaders are at a loss to explain this turnaround.

How very interesting. Perhaps the move from chocolate to blueberry was the result of changing attitudes to healthier living.

What do you mean it's more likely to do with the rate at which I consume them? Cheek!

Jack had warned me that Sarah Jardine had sounded

upset, but I hadn't expected her to be quite so distraught. We'd no sooner got into the lounge than she broke down in tears. It was several minutes before she managed to compose herself enough to talk.

"It's going to be okay, Sarah. We'll soon have this all cleared up."

"You don't understand. This is all my fault."

"Of course it isn't. It's just a misunderstanding. The police will soon realise their mistake."

"Bill and I had been seeing each other for the last three months."

I hadn't seen that one coming, and Jack obviously hadn't known anything about it, or he would have said something.

"Did your husband know?"

"I didn't think so, but he must have found out. Why else would he have done this?"

"You think he killed Bill?"

"Chris gets jealous if I so much as look at another man. If he had found out about Bill and me, then—" Her words trailed away.

"Have you mentioned any of this to the police?"

"No. I didn't even tell Jack, but they're bound to find out, aren't they?"

"Have you been able to speak to Chris since he was arrested?"

"Not yet, but our lawyer is trying to arrange something."

"So, you don't know for sure that your husband had found out about you and Bill?"

"No, but why else would he have killed him?"

"We can't be certain he did."

"They found traces of the poison on a cigarette that Chris gave to Bill, didn't they? What other explanation could there be?"

It was a good question, and not one that I had a ready answer for.

"When Chris came home on Tuesday, how did he seem?"

"I was already in bed, fast asleep, by the time he got back."

"What about the next morning?"

"He was still excited about the previous night's bowling victory. He never stopped talking about it."

"He wasn't acting in any way out of character?"

"No, he was fine until he heard that Bill had died."

"How did he hear?"

"He got a phone call."

"How did he react?"

"He was shocked, and very upset. At least, that's how it appeared at the time. Do you think I should contact the police and tell them about Bill and me?"

"If they ask you about it, then you'll have to tell the truth, but for now, let's see what happens with Chris."

As soon as I got back to the car, I called Jack.

"Sarah and Bill? I had no idea. I can't believe it."

"Do you think Chris could have known?"

"I don't see how he could have. He was just as pally with Bill as he ever was. When I left them on Tuesday, they were enjoying a cigarette and a laugh. Has Sarah told the Washbridge police about her and Bill?"

"Not yet, and I told her not to unless they specifically asked her about it. This doesn't look good, Jack. Chris had the motive and it was his cigarette that killed Bill."

"We need to hear Chris' side of the story. I'll try to arrange for you to see him."

"Okay."

***

I wasn't looking forward to breaking the news about the seating arrangements to my mother and father. When I'd told them that I was going to marry Jack, they'd both been super-excited, and adamant that they wanted to attend the ceremony and reception. Jack was right, though, there was no way that we could have what appeared to be an empty table next to the top table.

I decided to tackle my mother first. Once I'd explained the situation to her and Alberto, I'd mosey on down the road to talk to my father and Blodwyn.

At least, that had been the plan.

At first, I thought there was no one home at my mother's. I'd knocked a couple of times without response, but then I heard voices coming from around the back of the house.

Seated around a large table on the patio were my mother, father, Alberto and Blodwyn. They seemed to be having a whale of a time and didn't even notice my arrival.

"Hi, guys."

"Jill." My mother came over and gave me a hug. "What a pleasant surprise."

"I didn't expect to find you all together."

"We're having a barbecue. Or at least we will be later. We're just working our way through this bottle of wine first. Come and join us."

"Thanks. Hi, everyone."

My father gave me a hug, and then pulled up a chair for me.

"It's nice to see you're all getting along so well." I took a sip of the wine. "This is amazing. What is it?"

"Chateau Spook. Nineteen-fifty-seven." My father held up the bottle.

"How are your nerves, Jill?" Blodwyn asked. "It's not long now."

"Okay. I'm too busy to be nervous."

"We can't wait for the big day, can we, Blod?" my mother said. "We went shopping for our dresses last week. Would you like to see mine?"

"Not just now. It can be a surprise on the day."

"How's Jack doing?" Alberto asked.

"He's fine."

"Leaving you to see to all of the arrangements, I bet," my mother said.

"Actually, it's the wedding arrangements I need to talk to you about."

"There isn't a problem, is there?" My father looked concerned.

"Not a problem, exactly. It's just that we've run into a couple of minor hiccups regarding the seating."

"The seating plan is always the biggest headache." My mother finished the last of her wine. "Do you remember what a nightmare ours was, Alberto?"

He nodded.

"You know that we want you all to be there—at the ceremony and reception, but—err—well, it's just that you're going to have to sit at the back."

"At the back?" My mother looked horrified. "But we're the bride's parents."

"I know that, and under normal circumstances, you'd be right there at the front."

"What do you mean: *normal circumstances*?"

"If you weren't — how shall I put this? Dead."

"We may be dead, but I'll have you know I'm as fit as anyone who'll be at that wedding. I've started going to the gym, haven't I, Alberto?"

"You have, dear. Twice a week."

"That may be, but it doesn't alter the fact that you're — err — ghosts."

"What difference does that make?"

"Think about it. If you sit on the front row at the ceremony, I'll be the only person who can see you."

"You're the only one that matters."

"That's not the point. Everyone else will think those seats are empty. You'll end up with someone sitting on your lap."

"She has a point, Darlene," Alberto said.

"And at the reception, we can't have what appears to be an empty table at the front of the room. It was difficult enough for Jack to explain to the wedding planner why we need an extra table at all. You're going to have to sit at the back of the room, I'm afraid."

My mother frowned but said, "You're right. I'd like to be closer to you, but as long as I'm there, I don't mind."

"Don't worry about it, Jill," my father said. "We're going to love every minute of your big day, no matter where we have to sit."

"Thanks for understanding. That's a great weight off my mind."

Chapter 9

I'd arranged to talk to the CASS house captains about the missing trophy. First though, I called in at Cuppy C where Mindy and Amber were behind the counter. There weren't many customers in the tea room, but there were two workmen who were busy installing the new self-order machines.

"Morning, you two. I didn't realise they'd be installing your new machines this soon."

"It's exciting, isn't it?" Amber gushed. "We weren't supposed to get them until next month, but they had a last-minute cancellation."

"When will they be operational?"

"I'm hoping they'll be working later today, before I leave."

"Coffee, Jill?" Mindy said.

"No, thanks. I can't stay. I just called in to check if Amber was still on for the hen night."

"Just try stopping me. Alan's looking forward to having Lil all to himself for a change."

"What about Pearl? Is she coming?"

"Definitely. We've both bought new outfits, especially."

"You're welcome to come too, Mindy," I said.

"Thanks. It's kind of you to ask, but I promised to visit my parents on Saturday evening. And besides, I'm not sure I could keep pace with you three."

Amber came out from behind the counter. "Before you go, Jill, come and take a quick look at the self-order machines."

"They aren't wired up to the terminal yet, missus," one of the workmen said, as we approached.

"I know," Amber said. "I just want to show Jill what they look like."

"They're exactly like the ones in Burger Bay in Washbridge." I nodded my approval. "In fact, if I remember correctly, they've just had some new ones installed."

"Just look at the display." Amber pointed.

The on-screen menu showed small images of drinks and all manner of cakes.

"When they're working, you'll be able to order a blueberry muffin at the press of a button."

"I've actually given up blueberry muffins."

"Of course you have." She laughed.

"I have to admit that these machines are impressive."

"Didn't we tell you that this was our best idea yet?"

"You did, but then you've said that before. Have you forgotten the chocolate fountain and the conveyor belt? Not to mention the drive-thru and the —"

"Your problem, Jill, is you're too stuck in your ways."

"Rubbish."

"When was the last time you did anything innovative in your business?"

"Just last week, as it happens."

"Oh? And what was that?"

"I don't want to bore you with the details."

"Go on. I'm interested."

"I replaced my manual pencil sharpener with an electric one."

She dissolved into laughter.

"I'll have you know that it's dual-speed, and height adjustable."

For some reason, that just made her laugh even more.

Eventually, she recovered enough to carry on. "When are you coming over to see Lil again?"

"When would be convenient?"

"I'm going over to Pearl's place on Monday morning. Why don't you come then?"

"I will, thanks."

"Just one thing, Jill. Please don't mention how much prettier my Lil is than Amber's Lil. I wouldn't want to upset her."

"They're both gorgeous."

"I realise you have to say that, but a blind man could see my Lil is so much prettier."

"What time shall I come on Monday?"

"Pearl is coming over at ten."

"Okay. I'll be there just after ten."

"Hopefully, Pearl's Lil will behave this week. She must be a nightmare for Mum to look after. Not like my Lil — she's as good as gold — you never hear a peep out of her."

***

When I walked into the Nomad girls' dormitory, the four house captains: Toyah Harlow (Nomad), Lee Bartake (Longstaff), Belinda Postit (Wrongacre) and Gordon Reed (Capstan) were all seated at a table. Lee and Gordon both looked a little uncomfortable — perhaps it was their first time in the girls' dorm. At the head of the table was Mr Bluegrass, the deputy head.

"Thank you for coming, Jill." He gestured to the vacant seat at the far end of the table.

"No problem. I'm happy to help."

I'd no sooner taken my seat than something brushed

against my leg—I screamed and practically jumped out of the chair.

The four children all laughed.

"It's just Fluff, Miss," Lee Bartake said.

I glanced down to find the weird little creature that I'd encountered on my previous visit.

"Is it okay for him to be out of his cage?" I said.

"It certainly isn't." Mr Bluegrass did not look amused.

"Sorry, Sir." Felicity came running down the dorm. "The catch on his cage is wonky—it keeps popping open."

"Hurry up and catch him. We have important matters to discuss with Miss Gooder."

"Yes, Sir." Felicity scooped up Fluff and took him away.

"As I was saying before we were interrupted." The deputy head was clearly growing impatient. "The headmistress has asked Miss Gooder to come over today, to help to find the inter-house sports trophy."

"She should take a look in Toyah's locker then," Gordon Reed said.

"Shut up, Reedy!" Toyah glared at him.

"That's enough!" Mr Bluegrass thumped the table.

"Why would you think Toyah has the trophy, Gordon?" I asked.

"It's obvious, isn't it, Miss? Nomad are going to get trounced next week, and Harlow can't bear the thought of losing her precious cup."

"And your proof?"

"I—err—I just know she did it."

"So, no proof then?"

"Well no, but—"

"In that case, I suggest you keep your unfounded accusations to yourself." I turned to Toyah. "When did you last see the trophy?"

"Just before I turned in on Tuesday night."

"Where was it?"

"On there." She pointed to the bookcase.

"Is that where it's usually kept?"

"Most of the time, yes."

"And it was definitely there the night when it went missing?"

"Yes, Miss. Definitely."

Just then, I had a flashback to a similar incident that occurred about two years earlier. At that time, I'd been asked to investigate the disappearance of the Candlefield Cup, awarded to the winners of the BoundBall tournament.

"Does anyone have a mirror?"

"*Mirror?*" The deputy head looked puzzled.

"I have one in my locker." Toyah went to get it. "There you go, Miss."

"Thanks." I walked over to the bookcase and moved the mirror back and forth.

"I'm a little confused," the deputy head said. "What are you doing?"

"I worked on a case some time ago where a trophy had gone missing. It turned out that it was actually there all the time, but it had been hidden from sight by the 'hide' spell. I just wanted to rule that out this time." I returned the mirror to Toyah. "Is it possible that someone in your dorm could have taken the trophy as a lark?"

"Definitely not, Miss. Everyone in Nomad is very proud of having won the trophy. And besides, we're confident that we're going to retain it in next week's competition."

"In your dreams," Belinda Postit quipped. "Nomad will

be lucky not to finish last this year."

"You should check the Wrongacre dorms, Miss," Toyah said. "Belinda and two of her friends were in here on Tuesday."

I turned to Belinda. "Is that true?"

"I brought some of my team in here to look at the trophy, which we're going to win next week, but we didn't get a chance to see it because Toyah threatened to dob us in to the headmistress."

"You know you aren't allowed to enter another house's dorm," Mr Bluegrass said.

"Sorry, Sir."

"What about you, Lee?" I said. "You haven't had much to say yet."

"I don't think any of the pupils took the trophy, Miss. I know there's a lot of rivalry between the houses, but I just can't believe anyone would do something like that. The trophy is valuable, so surely it's possible that someone from outside the school stole it?"

"Like who?" Gordon scoffed. "It's not like anyone can get to CASS without being seen—the only access is by airship."

"Miss Gooder doesn't have to take the airship," Lee said.

"Are you suggesting that she stole it?"

"Of course not." Lee blushed. "I'm just saying that if Miss Gooder can magic herself here, maybe someone else can too."

He had a point. It was generally accepted that I was the only one capable of magicking myself back and forth between Candlefield and CASS, but what if there were others who could do it?

We talked for a while longer but didn't get very far.

"Okay," I said. "Let's leave it at that for now. I may need to speak to one or more of you individually, if that's okay?" I turned to the deputy head.

"Of course. The pupils and I are all at your disposal."

On my way out of the dormitory, Felicity came running over to me.

"Did you manage to find out anything about Fluff, Miss?"

"Not yet, I'm afraid."

"Please try, Miss. Time is running out."

***

After I'd left CASS, I got to thinking about what Lee Bartake had said. If there were others who could magic themselves between Candlefield and the school, then the gold thefts could be an outside job. If not, then it was almost certain to have been one of the pupils or a member of staff.

There was one person who might have the answers—someone who was always pleased to see me.

"What are you doing here?" Grandma came to the door in her dressing gown. She had curlers in her hair, and a horrible green cream plastered on her face.

"I thought I'd drop in to say hello."

"You never just *drop in*. Not unless you want something."

"That's a bit unfair."

"Do you want something or not? I'm in the middle of a pamper session."

"What's that horrible stuff on your face?"

"It's my secret-recipe anti-ageing cream. How else do you think I stay looking this young? I'm thinking of starting a new business to sell it. I could call it Ever Young."

"I'm not sure that's such a good idea."

"Why not? There's a massive market for this kind of thing. I bet you'd be all over it."

"Me?" I touched my forehead. "I don't have any wrinkles."

"I've always admired your capacity for self-delusion, Jill. Now, if you don't mind, I need to—"

"Actually, there was something I wanted to ask you."

"I knew it. You'd better make it snappy because I have to get this cream off before it sets hard. The last time I put it on, I fell asleep, and had to use a chisel to chip it off."

"I just wanted to ask if you thought it was possible that anyone apart from me could magic themselves to CASS."

"No." She began to close the door.

"Hold on. Don't you need to think about it?"

"No."

"Grandma, this is important."

"And I've already given you my answer. If anyone else could do it, it would be me, and I can't. I've tried."

"But, maybe someone else—"

"Are you suggesting that there's someone, apart from you, who is more powerful or skilful than me?"

"Well, err—no, of course not."

"Then you have your answer. What's this all about, anyway?"

"There's been a spate of robberies at CASS—gold jewellery. Everyone assumes it's an inside job, but if someone could magic themselves there and back, then it might be an outsider."

"It's probably one of the teachers. I never did trust the teaching profession."

"That's a bit harsh."

"You know what they say. Those who can, do. Those who can't, become jewel thieves. Now, if you don't mind, I need to take this cream off." She slammed the door in my face.

"Bye, Grandma."

As I walked back down the path, Aunt Lucy appeared next door.

"Jill! I thought I saw you there. Can you spare me a minute? I've just brewed a pot of tea."

"Sure."

Once seated in the lounge, Aunt Lucy passed me a new packet of custard creams. Now that I'd given up on muffins, I didn't feel guilty about helping myself to a couple.

"Is four enough, Jill?"

What? I know I said I'd taken a couple, but everyone knows that a *couple* can mean any number between two and six. Duh!

"Did your grandmother summon you?"

"No. I was picking her brain, actually. I wanted to know if she thought anyone else could magic themselves back and forth to CASS. She said she didn't."

"You weren't around there for very long."

"She was in the middle of a pamper session."

"Did she have that horrible cream on her face?"

"Yeah. She reckons she might start to sell it."

"Oh dear. I hope she doesn't decide to star in the

adverts herself. No one will ever buy it if she does."

"Harsh but true." I took a sip of tea. "You are coming on the hen night on Saturday, aren't you?"

"You don't want an oldie like me there."

"Of course I do, and besides, Mad's mother is coming."

"The twins wouldn't want me there."

"It doesn't matter what they want. It's my hen night and I want you to come."

"It is rather a long time since I let my hair down and had a dance."

"That's settled then. Get your glad rags on and meet us at Kathy's house at eight o'clock."

"I think I will."

"Will you come with the twins?"

"No, I'd rather surprise them." She grinned. "Anyway, the main reason I called you in is that Barry said he wanted a word the next time I saw you."

"Is he okay?"

"Yeah, he's fine. He and his new tortoise friend seem to be getting on like a house on fire."

"Where is Barry?"

"He's in the back garden with the tortoise."

"Jill!" Barry came bounding over to me.

"Don't jump up with those muddy —" Too late.

"I'm playing with Rhymes."

"The tortoise? I thought his name was Dimes."

"No, it's definitely Rhymes. He's called that because he's a poet. Come and see." Barry led the way across the lawn. "Rhymes, this is Jill."

Rhymes looked up (slowly). "Greetings. I apologise for sleeping through our last meeting."

"That's okay. I'm sorry I got your name wrong. Barry tells me you're a poet."

"Indeed I am."

"Read Jill the poem you wrote for me," Barry said.

"Certainly." He cleared his little tortoise throat.

"Barry is a dog.
Not a chicken or a cow or a hog.
Barkies are his favourite food.
He never gives me one but that isn't rude.
Because I only eat plants.
And I think Barkies are pants."

"That's — err — very good."

"Thank you."

"He's written a poem for you too, Jill." Barry's tail was wagging with excitement. "Haven't you, Rhymes?"

"Barry told me you were getting married next week, so I thought this poem could be my present to you." He reached into his shell and pulled out a piece of paper. "There you are."

"Thanks. That's — err — very kind."

"Read it, Jill," Barry said.

"Okay." I unfolded the paper.

"Jill is a witch.
She may not be tall, but don't call her titch.
To a human named Jack she's going to get wed.
He's very handsome, at least that's what she said.
The happy couple will be covered in confetti
Let's hope it's not too hot so she doesn't get sweaty."

Chapter 10

When I arrived back at the office, Mrs V was standing next to the wall opposite her desk.

"Jill, you've timed it just right. Would you hold this, please?" She handed me a tape measure, and then pulled the tape across the wall. "I want to know how wide it needs to be."

"How wide *what* needs to be?"

"The tapestry of course."

Sometimes, it felt like I'd stepped into a parallel universe.

"What tapestry?"

"I thought I'd mentioned it to you."

"I think I would have remembered a conversation about a tapestry."

"Since I moved my desk, I've been forced to stare at a blank wall all day. That's how I came up with the idea of a tapestry. It won't be a conventional one, obviously."

"Obviously."

"I thought I'd knit one. The theme will be this business, so you'll be centre stage, of course."

"Right. I assume you'll be on there, too?"

"Yes, but only in the background."

"And Winky?"

"Definitely not." She looked appalled at the idea.

"It will certainly be a talking-point once it's finished. How long do you think it will take you?"

"I'm not really sure. A long time."

"The old bag lady really hates me, doesn't she?" Winky said, as soon as I went through to my office.

"What makes you say that?"

"I heard what she said just now. How can you have a tapestry based on this place without yours truly on it?"

"Why do you care?"

"It's the principle that matters."

"Never mind about that. Why are you wearing a sailor's uniform?"

"Do you like it? It's the latest fashion: Marine Chic."

"I can't say I've noticed anyone wearing *marine chic*."

"Let's get real here. It's not like you move in haute couture circles, do you?" He looked me up and down. "When was the last time you updated your wardrobe?"

"I don't follow fashion. I prefer to go for the classic, timeless look."

"Of course you do." He laughed. "You really should allow me to give you a few fashion tips."

"When I ask for fashion advice from a cat, I'll know it's time to call the men with white coats."

Just then, my office door opened.

"Looks like they're already here." He laughed.

It was actually Mrs V.

"Why do you dress that cat up like that?" She stared at him in disbelief.

"I — err — "

"What's he meant to be this time? A pilot?"

"It's marine chic."

She rolled her eyes. "I'd have thought you needed to watch your pennies with the wedding coming up. Does Jack know you buy clothes for the cat?"

"Did you want something, Mrs V?"

"Madeline Lane is here. Do you have time to see her?"

"Mad? Of course. Send her through, please."

"I should warn you, Jill. I don't think London suits her."

"How do you mean?"

"I hate to say it, but she seems to have let herself go a little. You'll see for yourself."

"Hiya, Jill." Mad gave me a hug. "I've missed you."

"Likewise." I grinned. "Mrs V thinks you've let yourself go."

"Oh dear. Did I shock her?"

"She's used to seeing you dressed as a librarian, so she wasn't expecting this punk rocker look."

"What do you think of it?"

"I like it. This is more like the Mad I used to know. I'm guessing you're no longer working as a librarian."

"No, thank goodness. I managed to wangle a cover-job in a boutique on Carnaby Street. It's only a small place, but we sell some great gear. You should definitely check it out when you come down to London next."

"I don't really think I'm your target demographic. How did you manage to get that gig? It doesn't sound like the kind of job they usually expect you to take as cover for the ghost-hunting."

"Now I've proven myself as a ghost hunter, I get a bit more say in the cover job I take. It's like I told my bosses, I stood out like a sore thumb in the library just because I was so far out of my comfort zone. In this job, I fit right in."

"I can believe that. Anyway, I'm glad you managed to get up here in time for the hen night."

"I wasn't going to miss that for the world. We'll have a ball."

"Your mum's looking forward to it."

"Mum? You haven't invited her, have you?"

"I assumed you knew."

"I haven't seen her yet. I came straight here from the station. I knew she was going to the wedding, but what possessed you to invite her on the hen do?"

"She pretty much invited herself."

"Oh well, I'll just have to steer clear of her. I don't want her showing me up."

"Her nail business seems to be doing really well."

"So I hear, which reminds me, I promised to drop in on her, so I'd better get going."

"See you on Saturday, Mad."

***

My feet had barely touched the ground all day, whizzing back and forth between Washbridge, Candlefield and Ghost Town.

It was supposed to be my turn to make dinner, but once Jack heard about my hectic day, I was sure he'd volunteer to step into the breach.

All I wanted to do was to get in the house, kick off my shoes and relax in front of the TV.

"Hi, Jill," the giant burger shouted when I got out of the car.

"Hi, Tony."

"I see you've got a new next-door neighbour." This came from the giant hotdog who was standing next to the burger.

"Hi, Clare. Yes, his name is Ivers. We've known each other for some time, actually."

"That's lucky. It's always a bit of a worry, wondering

who your new neighbours might turn out to be. No one wants to live next door to some weirdos."

So said the giant burger.

"Mr Ivers is really nice," I said. "You should go around there and introduce yourselves. It wouldn't surprise me if he'd be up for cosplay. He's game for most things."

What? Of course I was going to throw them under the bus if it got Ivers off my back.

Snigger.

"That's a great idea," Tony said. "We're always on the lookout for new blood. It's a pity you and Jack aren't able to come with us more often."

"We'd love to. You know that. It's just that we're both so busy, what with the wedding and everything."

"We were gutted we couldn't make it to your wedding," Clare said. "But we'd already committed to CheeseCon that weekend. It's the same every year: FastFoodCon one weekend and CheeseCon the next. We've suggested they split them up because it can get tiresome, dressing up as food for two consecutive weeks, but they don't seem to take any notice of us."

"I can see how that must be tedious. Anyway, I'd better get going because I have dinner to make. Don't forget to introduce yourselves to Mr Ivers."

"Jill, we're in here," Jack called from the lounge.

We? Who was the *we*?

The sight that greeted me was so shocking that my legs almost gave way. Only by holding onto the door frame did I manage to stay upright.

Jack seemed not to notice my distress. "This is Jimmy and Kimmy — our new neighbours from across the road."

Seated on the sofa were two clowns.

I tried to speak but was paralysed by fear.

"Are you okay?" the taller of the two said.

"Err—yeah, sorry. I haven't eaten for a while. I just went a little light-headed, that's all. I'm okay now."

"I thought for a moment it might be our fault," the shorter clown said. "You'll probably be surprised to hear that there are some people who are afraid of clowns."

"Really?" I feigned shock.

The tall clown stood up and offered his hand.

I hesitated, but then realised how ridiculous I was being.

"Nice to meet you," I said, but immediately pulled away when the electric shock hit me.

"Sorry." He laughed. "Old habits die hard." He squeezed his red nose and made it squeak.

"That's okay," I said through gritted teeth.

"We were just on our way to a gig when Jack called us over." He checked his comedy watch. "We really must get going. Come on, Sneezy."

His partner pulled herself to her feet—her giant clown's feet.

Jack saw them to the door; I followed at a safe distance behind.

"I thought you said their names were Jimmy and Kimmy?" I said after they'd left.

"Those are their real names. Breezy and Sneezy are their stage names."

"Why did you invite them in?"

"It's the neighbourly thing to do."

"I thought you said they were something in show

business."

"Clowns are show business, aren't they?"

"No, they're pure evil." I slumped onto the sofa. "After that nasty shock, the least you could do is make dinner."

"Okay, but that's one you owe me."

"Of course, my darling."

Just then, there was a knock at the door.

"If it's the clowns, don't let them back in," I shouted.

"It's Peter. Come on in."

"Are you okay, Jill?" Peter asked. "You look pale."

"I'm fine. I've just gone too long without anything to eat. Jack was just about to make dinner."

"Do you want to join us?" Jack asked.

"No, thanks. I just popped over on my way home to take a look at the sandpit. This really is a weird neighbourhood you live in. When I got out of the van, there were two clowns across the road. And there's a giant burger and hotdog talking to your next-door neighbour. It makes our street look positively boring."

"I'll show you the garden." I pulled myself up off the sofa. "While Jack makes a start on dinner."

"Are you sure you want to get rid of this?" Peter studied the sandpit. "You haven't had it long."

"Positive. The kids obviously aren't that bothered about it, and it will be nice to get our garden back."

"What were you thinking of having in its place?"

"Just a small lawn, and flowerbeds. Nothing too elaborate."

"Okay. It shouldn't be much of a job. I should be able to fit it in within the next two to three weeks."

"Great. How much will it cost us?"

"Kathy came up with a good suggestion. We haven't got around to buying you guys a wedding present yet, so why don't we call this it?"

"Sounds good to me if you're okay with that."

"Definitely."

"Hello, Jill!" Mr Ivers called from over the fence.

"Oh, hello, Mr Ivers."

"Now we're neighbours, you must call me Monty." He glanced at Peter. "Aren't you going to introduce me, Jill?"

"Sorry. This is Peter, my brother-in-law. Peter, this is Mr Ivers, our new next-door neighbour."

"Pleased to meet you, Peter," Mr Ivers said.

"Likewise." Peter shook hands with him.

"I've just been talking to your other neighbours. This cosplay thing sounds fascinating. I'm going to join them for CheeseCon. I would have gone to FastFoodCon too, but apparently all the tickets have already been sold."

"Peter's here to look at the sandpit—we're wanting to get rid of it. He has his own landscaping business."

"Really?" He turned back to Peter. "I have my own business too. Do you like movies?"

Before I could warn him, Peter said, "I do enjoy a good film."

"In that case, this is your lucky day."

***

I was still chuckling to myself over dinner, long after Peter had left.

"You really dropped poor old Peter in it," Jack said.

"It wasn't my fault. He was the one who said he enjoyed movies. And anyway, he got fifty percent discount for being Ivers' first ever customer."

"Kathy will kill you."

"She can't, or she won't get to be a bridesmaid."

Jack was quiet for the rest of the meal.

"Are you okay?" I said.

"Yeah. I was just thinking about poor old Chris, locked up behind bars."

"Have you heard back from his solicitor yet?"

"Not yet. He said he'd try and get back to me tonight or in the morning. You'll need to be ready to go and see him at a moment's notice."

"No problem. Chris is my number one priority."

"I still can't believe that Sarah and Bill were having a fling."

"Do you think Chris knew about it?"

"If he did, he hid it well because he acted the same way towards Bill as he always has."

Chapter 11

For once, when I arrived at the office, Mrs V wasn't knitting.

"Why won't this stupid thing work?" She sighed.

"Is that *your* phone, Mrs V?"

"Yes. Armi bought it for me yesterday. I wanted a cerise one, but they only had white or black."

"I didn't have you down as a smart phone kind of a person."

"Why? Because I'm getting on a bit? I still have all my faculties, you know."

"I didn't mean that. I know you have. I've just never seen you with a mobile phone before."

"I'm not really a fan, but when I heard about the wap your grandmother had made, I had to get one."

"What's a—oh, hang on. Are you talking about an *app*?"

"Wap? App? Why do they have to use jargon? I heard that it would be available today, but I can't see it on here." She handed the phone to me.

"Have you actually installed it?"

"Installed what?"

"The wap—err—app?"

"How do I do that?"

"You have to go to the app store."

She sighed again, even more exasperated this time. "Where's that? I didn't realise I'd have to go running around town."

"The app store isn't actually a store. Well, it is a store, but—"

"It's all too complicated. Could you do it for me, Jill?"

"I'm not all that great with phones myself."

"How disappointing. I was so looking forward to trying it."

"Don't worry. I know someone who's a whizz with phones. Can I hang onto this for a while?"

"Do you think your friend will be able to do it for me today?"

"That depends if there's any salmon."

"Sorry?"

"Err—I said it depends on Sam Dunn. That's my friend. It depends how busy he is."

"Okay, well please do your best. I've been really looking forward to this."

Winky was rolling around the floor, in hysterics.

"What's so funny?"

"Sam Dunn? How do you come up with this stuff?"

"You shouldn't be tabby-hanging."

"It's hard not to when you're shouting at the old bag lady."

"You know Mrs V is hard of hearing."

"Pardon?"

"I said—oh, very funny."

"I take it you want me to install a *wap* on her phone?"

"Yes, please."

"Tinder?"

"Don't be ridiculous. It's something to do with knitting."

"What's it called?"

"I don't remember. I suggested Grandma call it Copy Cat, but she didn't like that name."

"Whoa, back up. Why would you make such a slur?"

"What are you talking about?"

"You appear to be insinuating that cats have no originality. That they steal the ideas of others and claim them as their own."

"*Copycat*? That's just a saying. It doesn't mean anything."

"Then why not say copy dog?"

"That doesn't alliterate."

"Okay. Copy koala, then."

"That begins with a 'K'."

"How about copy cobra? Those pesky snakes are notorious for their counterfeit activities."

"Okay, if it makes you happy, I'll say copy cobra from now on."

"Good. So, what's this app called?"

"I remember now. It's called: See It. Make It. A stupid name if you ask me."

"I think it's a great name. I'm not sure you should be questioning your grandmother's nous for marketing, given her track record compared to yours."

Touché. "Will you install the app or not?"

"Depends how much Sam Dunn you had in mind."

"You can have salmon today and tomorrow."

"And all next week."

"Okay, okay. Just install the stupid app."

He did his thing, and less than a couple of minutes later, handed the phone back to me. "All done. There's a shortcut on the home screen."

"Thank you."

"Hey, while I remember. Do I get to travel to the wedding ceremony in the limousines with you guys?"

"Err—sorry, but there's no room. You're going to have to make your own way there."

"Fair enough. Where's the wedding taking place?"

There was no way I could allow Winky to walk down the aisle as my pagecat. If I did, I'd be a laughing stock. This might be my only chance to do something about it without hurting his feelings. If I gave him the name of the wrong hotel, by the time he realised, it would be too late, and the ceremony would be over. Was I a genius or what?

I wasn't asking for your opinion. Don't you recognise a rhetorical question when you hear one? Right there—that was another one.

"It's at the Washbridge Hotel at two o'clock."

"Got it. I'll be there."

Snigger.

Back in the outer office, I handed Mrs V her phone.

"All done. The app is installed. Look, it's there on the home screen."

"I thought you said you'd have to get your friend, Sam Dunn, to install it?"

"I—err managed to do it myself."

"Thank you. Do you think you could show me how it works?"

Just then, my phone rang; Jack had managed to arrange for me to visit Chris Jardine in prison.

***

Chris was being held on remand at Longdale Prison, which was a thirty-mile drive from Washbridge. Although I didn't relish the thought of visiting the prison, it did at least give me an excuse to leave Mrs V to try to sort out her new app by herself.

"Is it true about Sarah and Bill?" Were the first words out of Chris Jardine's mouth.

"Mr Jardine, this is Jill Gooder," the solicitor said. "I believe you're expecting her."

"Yes, sorry." Chris slumped onto the metal chair. "You're Jack's wife, aren't you?"

"No, yes, well almost. We're getting married next week."

"Was Sarah really having an affair with Bill?"

"I'm afraid so." I nodded. "She told me so herself."

At that, he broke down in tears. I'd never been comfortable around people when they cried, and for some reason, it seemed even worse when it was a man.

"I realise this is hard for you, Chris." I passed him a tissue. "But, if I'm going to help you, I'll need to ask you a few questions about your relationship with Bill, and the events of Tuesday night."

"Sorry." He took a deep breath and wiped his eyes. "This has all come as such a shock. I thought Sarah and I were solid. And I thought Bill was a friend."

"Had you noticed any change in your wife's behaviour recently?"

"Nothing. Nothing at all."

"Can you talk me through what happened on Tuesday night?"

"It was a great night. At least, I thought so at the time. Jack and I beat Bill and Graham for the first time. Jack must have told you about it."

"He did, but I'd still like to hear it from you."

"Graham had to leave a couple of frames before the end, but we already had it sewn up at that point."

"Do you know why he had to leave?"

"He got a phone call to say his brother had been taken into hospital, I think."

"What happened after the match was over?"

"After Jack left, Bill and I had a cigarette in the car park as usual. Then Bill left, and that was the last time I saw him."

"Did you give Bill the cigarette?"

"Yes. He never had any of his own because he was supposed to have given them up."

"And you smoked a cigarette from the same packet?"

"That's right. I know the police reckon I put poison on Bill's cigarette, but that's rubbish. I had no reason to kill him because I had no idea that he was seeing Sarah."

"How did Bill seem when he left you?"

"Okay. As soon as we'd finished our cigarettes, we said goodnight and went our separate ways."

***

I'd promised to try to identify Fluff, but I was going to need some help. It occurred to me that Mr Shuttlebug's widow might still have his unpublished manuscript, so I gave her a call.

"You've reached the Shuttlebug residence. Deloris Shuttlebug speaking. I'm unable to take your call because I'm away from home for a few days. I will be back on Tuesday."

Disappointing, but I'd just have to try again then. That wouldn't leave long until the deadline for identifying the strange little creature, but I had no other bright ideas.

Mrs V and I were due to attend the grand opening of The Sea's The Limit, so I called into the office to collect her on the way past.

"I've got it working, Jill." She looked very pleased with herself about something.

"Got *what* working?"

"The wap. It's very straightforward."

"Good. Come on. We'd better get a move on."

"Where are we going?"

"It's the grand opening of The Sea's The Limit. Had you forgotten?"

"I'm afraid I had. It's all the excitement of my new phone. Shall I bring it with me?"

"If you like."

"I think I will. I may see a nice jumper while we're out."

"You're late, Jill." Betty was standing by the entrance to The Sea's The Limit.

"Sorry, I lost track of time."

"All of the best seats have already gone, I'm afraid. There are just a few left on the back row."

"I'm sure they'll be fine."

"Follow me." She led the way inside. "We've managed to get Finn Waters to do the honours."

"Who?"

"You must have heard of him. Finn does all those marine life documentaries." She pointed to the few empty seats at the back of the large room, which contained two enormous tanks. "You'll have to sit over there."

"Okay. How come only one of the tanks has any fish in it?"

"The dangerous species will go in that tank, but we haven't received the licence for them yet. We didn't want to wait any longer—there have been enough delays already."

"Is that Sid?" I pointed to the scuba diver in the tank that had no fish in it.

"It is. Sorry, Jill, I have to go and introduce Finn."

"Okay. Good luck, Betty."

Moments after Mrs V and I had taken our seats, Betty appeared on the small makeshift stage, accompanied by a short, stout man.

"Look at his jumper." Mrs V nudged me.

"It's horrible."

"I think it's nice." She took out her phone and snapped a photo.

"Ladies and gentlemen." Betty spoke into the mic. "Thank you for coming here today. Without further ado, it's my great pleasure to welcome Finn Waters."

"Thank you, Betty." He took the mic. from her. "It is a great honour to be asked here to open The Sea's The Limit. I'm pleased to confirm that the giftshop will be stocking my range of marine-themed jumpers and cardigans." He pointed to his own jumper. "They're available in all sizes, including children's."

"He's just here to flog his horrible knitwear," I whispered to Mrs V.

But I was wrong. He was there to bore us all to death for the next forty-five minutes, with talk of crustaceans and fish. By the time he'd finished, I was practically asleep.

"And so." He picked up a magnum of champagne. "It gives me great pleasure to declare The Sea's The Limit open." He smashed the bottle on the tank closest to him.

And then it happened. At first, it was just a tiny crack in the glass, but that quickly spread. I glanced at Betty and could tell by the look of horror on her face that all was not well.

"Quick, Mrs V." I grabbed her by the arm.

"What's wrong?"

"Hurry up. We have to get out of here."

We'd just reached the exit when I heard what sounded like a small explosion behind us.

"Jill, I really shouldn't be running like this."

"You have to." I managed to drag her across the road and into EAWM. "Quick. Upstairs."

"By the time we reached the top of the stairs, poor old Mrs V was gasping for air. "What was that all about?" She slumped onto one of the sun loungers on the roof terrace.

"Look!" I pointed to the road.

"Oh dear. That's dreadful."

Below us, a torrent of water was cascading down the street. Moments later, dozens of disgruntled people appeared — they were all soaked to the skin. In the middle of them was Betty who was trying her best to placate the angry crowd.

"What happened?" Mrs V had just about recovered.

"The tank broke when he hit it with the bottle."

"Surely, that shouldn't have happened?"

"It definitely shouldn't have happened, but I do recall that Betty said they'd managed to get those tanks much cheaper than she'd expected."

"It's like I always say, Jill. You get what you pay for."

Once the water had subsided, I walked Mrs V back to the office.

"Aren't you coming in, Jill?"

"I'm going to call it a day. It's my hen night tomorrow,

so I want to conserve my energy for that. I thought I'd give myself the rest of the day off."

"Okay, dear. Don't drink too much tomorrow night."

"Don't worry. I have no intention of doing. Are you sure you wouldn't like to join us?"

"Goodness, no." She laughed. "My hen night days are well and truly behind me."

"Okay, See you on Monday, then."

***

I'd gone cold turkey for far too long. If I didn't have a blueberry muffin soon, I'd get the screaming abdabs, so before heading home, I magicked myself to my favourite muffin emporium (and coincidentally, the only one that gave me a discount).

"Jill, you've timed it just right," Amber said.

"Isn't it supposed to be your day off?"

"It is, but I couldn't miss the launch of our new self-order machines."

"They've just finished commissioning them." Pearl joined her sister behind the counter. "I gave Amber a call because I knew she'd want to be here to see them in action."

"Where's your Lil, Amber?"

"I dropped her off at Mum's."

"You'll wear poor old Aunt Lucy out."

"I'll only be here an hour or so, and besides Mum loves it. It's not like *my* Lil is any trouble."

If Pearl picked up on the subtle dig, she didn't react. She was much too enthralled with the machines. "You can be the first person to place an order with them, Jill."

"I just popped in for a blueberry muffin and a caramel latte."

"I know. Go and place your order on the machine."

"But I've just told you what I want."

"Come on, Jill. It'll be fun."

"Won't it just." I walked over to the machine closest to me. I was already familiar with the format, having used them in Burger Bay. I selected the muffin first, and then the drink. "Right, I've done it."

"You have to pay before the order comes through to us."

"Where's the slot for the card?"

Amber laughed. "There isn't one."

"Why not?" And then I remembered that there were no credit or debit cards in Candlefield.

"You have to pay with cash," Pearl shouted.

"Okay." I slipped some coins into the slot. "There. Done it."

Amber and Pearl were both staring at the small terminal behind the counter.

"Is anything happening?" I shouted.

"Not yet."

"It's very slow, isn't it?"

"Have some patience—here it comes now!" Amber shrieked.

"Let me!" Pearl tore off the slip before Amber could get to it.

"Didn't we tell you that these machines would be brilliant?" Amber said.

I didn't reply. I was too busy looking at the expression on Pearl's face. "What's up, Pearl?"

"Did you order a burger?"

"Of course I didn't. You don't sell them."

"What about a strawberry milkshake?"

"I ordered a muffin and a latte. Why?"

"What's wrong?" Amber snatched the slip from her sister. "This can't be right."

I walked over to the counter and took the slip from Amber.

"Oh dear. Have you seen the tiny print at the bottom? It says, Burger Bay."

"What?" Pearl grabbed the slip from my hand.

"I told you that Burger Bay had just had some new machines installed. It looks like someone has sold you their old ones."

"But they said they'd be reconditioned and re-programmed specifically for our shop."

"It seems like the only changes they've made are the images on screen. I'm sorry to say this, girls, but I think you've been conned."

Chapter 12

It was Saturday — the day of my hen night. Yippee!

I'd never been a fan of hen nights — they were just so juvenile. What could be more embarrassing than a bunch of grown women, parading around town, wearing silly costumes and hats? Well, not mine. I'd made it quite clear to Kathy and the twins that I was having none of that. If I had to have a hen night, then mine would be a classy affair.

What do you mean, famous last words?

Jack was much more enthusiastic about his stag night. His best man, Alby, had been organising it for weeks, apparently. Fortunately, they were going to West Chipping, so we wouldn't have to worry about the two groups bumping into one another.

"Please tell me that you aren't going to walk around West Chipping wearing those things?" I said.

Jack and Alby were sporting brand new bowling shirts with the words 'Team Groom' printed on the back.

"What's wrong with them?" Alby looked affronted. "I designed them myself."

"I don't doubt it."

"I wasn't sure about them at first," Jack said. "But they've grown on me."

"Just as well." Alby picked up a cardboard box from under the kitchen table. "I've had a load of them printed."

"How many people are going on your do?" I said.

"I'm not sure." Jack shrugged.

"Twenty-six," Alby said. "Twenty-seven if Tommo makes it. He had to have an in-grown toenail removed yesterday, so it'll be touch and go. How many are going on your hen night, Jill?"

"Not many. It's going to be a small, but classy affair."

They both grinned.

"It will. I've spoken to Kathy and the twins, and they know I don't want anything loud or tacky."

"Good luck with that." Alby laughed.

***

We'd all arranged to meet at Kathy's house. Peter had taken the kids to his mother's, and from there he would be going straight to West Chipping to meet up with the other guys.

"Men are so juvenile," I said.

"Have you only just worked that one out?" Kathy was putting on her makeup. She'd always been so much better at doing it than I was. I just didn't have the patience.

"Alby has had a load of bowling shirts printed with 'Team Groom' on the back."

"What's wrong with that?" Kathy laughed. "It is a stag night."

"They're supposed to be grown men."

"Men never grow up. Surely, you've learned that much by now."

"You wouldn't catch me walking around town, wearing something as tacky as that."

"What time did you say the twins are coming over?"

Before I could answer, there was a knock at the door.

"That's probably them."

It wasn't—it was Aunt Lucy.

"Am I too early?"

"Of course not. Come on in. Kathy's just getting ready. Would you like a drink?"

"Not yet. I don't want to get tipsy too soon."

"I meant tea or coffee."

"Oh, right." She laughed. "A cup of tea would be nice."

"Come through to the kitchen. We can chat in there while Kathy tries to do something with her face. It could take her a while."

Aunt Lucy shot me a disapproving look.

"I'm only joking. We're always teasing one another. Did you tell the twins you were coming tonight?"

"No, I thought I'd let that be a surprise. I do have a message from your grandmother, though."

"She hasn't changed her mind, has she?"

"No, you can relax. She said she was sorry she couldn't make it tonight, but she has her bridge club."

"Thank goodness for bridge."

A few minutes later, Kathy came through to the kitchen. "Is there a cup of tea in the pot for me?"

"I'll pour you one." Aunt Lucy made to get up.

"Stay where you are, Lucy," Kathy said. "I'll see to it."

"I thought you were going to put your makeup on," I quipped.

"I have put—oh, very funny. I notice *you* didn't offer to pour me a cup of tea."

"Have you forgotten? This is my special day. Everyone is supposed to pamper to *my* needs."

As Kathy was pouring herself a cup of tea, there was another knock at the door.

"I'll get it." I volunteered.

It was the twins.

"I like your dresses. They're identical, aren't they?"

"I bought mine first," Amber said.

"No, you didn't," Pearl snapped. "I've had mine for weeks."

"Why didn't you tell me, then?"

"I didn't realise I needed to."

"Girls, girls! Not tonight, please."

"Sorry, Jill," they chorused.

"Come on through. We're in the kitchen."

"Mum?" Amber glared at Aunt Lucy. "What are you doing here?"

"Going on Jill's hen night, the same as you two."

"But you're too old," Pearl said.

"Thanks very much."

"You said you weren't going to come," Amber said.

"Jill persuaded me to change my mind."

The twins both glared at me.

"There's no reason why Aunt Lucy shouldn't come with us. It's not like this is going to be some kind of wild night. Just a few drinks and good conversation."

The twins were still sulking when someone else came to the door.

"Mad. You look very—err, normal. For you, that is."

"I thought, seeing as how it was *your* hen night, I'd better tone it down a little."

"Thanks. Like I was just saying to the twins, this is going to be a very low-key affair."

"Yeah, err—about that. There's something I need to tell you."

"What's that?"

Before she could reply, someone shouted, "If it isn't the blushing bride herself." It was Deli. "Hiya, Jill. Are you ready to tear up the town?" She took a swig from the half-empty bottle of gin in her hand.

I'd try to describe her outfit, but there aren't words that could begin to do it justice. Let's just say that there were bits of her on display that really shouldn't have been.

"Where is everyone?" She pushed past us and made her way through to the kitchen. "There you all are. Why are you drinking tea? This is supposed to be a hen night."

I turned to Mad. "What are those in her hand?"

Before Mad could reply, Deli held up the stack of witch's hats—PINK witch's hats! "Look what I've got for us."

"Sorry, Jill," Mad said. "I tried to stop her."

"Who wants one?" Deli said.

"I don't think we—" I began.

"Me!" Pearl yelled.

"I'll have one," Amber said.

"Count me in." Kathy grabbed one too.

Even though Aunt Lucy and Mad had remained silent, Deli handed them both a hat, and then she turned to me. "This one is for you, Jill."

"I don't really think—"

"Put it on!" Deli began to chant; the twins and Kathy soon joined in. "Put it on! Put it on!"

"Okay, okay." I put the stupid hat onto my head. "Why did you get *witches'* hats?"

"I had intended to get cowgirl hats, but these were on special offer."

"Why pink, though?"

"It's all they had left. They look good, don't they?"

I wasn't overly thrilled about the hat, but I supposed I could just about live with it.

"And this is for you too, Jill." Deli held up a T-shirt.

"I'm not wearing that thing!"

But of course, I did, and the humiliation was complete.

The giant 'L' plate on the back was bad enough, but it was what was on the front that was beyond the pale.

What? No, it wasn't that. Sheesh, your mind.

In big, bold words it said: I'm the bride. Please buy me a drink.

"Keeping it classy, I see." Kathy laughed. We were all on our way into Washbridge in two taxis.

"Shut up!"

"Look at the positive side. You probably won't have to buy any drinks all night."

"You look stupid in that hat," I said.

"I think it suits me. I've always thought I'd make a good witch."

We kicked off the evening in what had once been called Bar Fish until it rebranded to Bar Piranha. It was some time since I'd last been in there, and I was quite surprised to find it had undergone yet another transformation. It was now called Bubbles, and it wasn't difficult to work out why. I've never been a big fan of bubbles. When we were kids, Kathy spent hours blowing the things, but I could never see the point. All that effort, and two minutes later, they'd all burst.

"It's great in here, isn't it?" Amber said.

"I could do without all the stupid bubbles."

"I love them." Pearl took a sip from her purple cocktail.

"I'm not sure it was necessary to have twenty-six bubble machines," I said. "Two would have been plenty."

"I can't believe you've counted them." Kathy's cocktail was bright orange.

"What would you like to drink, love?" A man, with more hair sticking out of his nostrils than on his head, pointed to my T-shirt.

"I'm okay." I held up my glass. "Thanks, anyway."

I'd told the barman to make me a lime and soda, but to put in a little umbrella so I could pass it off as a cocktail.

"If you change your mind, I'll be just over there." Nose-hair gave me a wink.

I turned to Kathy. "See! I told you this T-shirt was a stupid idea."

"Relax and try to enjoy yourself. You only get married once. Hopefully."

I hadn't seen Aunt Lucy for a while, but then I spotted her. Deli had her cornered near to the bar. I probably should have gone and rescued her, but then I'd have been stuck with Deli.

Some sacrifices were just too great.

I'd managed to find a quiet spot, to one side of the bar. It was out of range of the bubble machines, and if I faced the wall, no one could see the front of my T-shirt.

"Shot time!" Deli appeared behind me. "Come on, Jill. We're moving onto shots."

"I'm okay with this cocktail."

"Nonsense. A hen night isn't a hen night without shots." She grabbed me by the hand and led me over to where everyone else was waiting. In front of them, on the bar, was a line of shots. "Okay, everyone. On three. One, two, three."

Everyone threw back their shot. Everyone except me, that is. I threw mine over my shoulder.

"Another round of shots, barman!" Deli demanded.

Moments later, we repeated the exercise. Everyone downed their shot except for me. Once again, mine went over my shoulder.

"Hey!" someone yelled.

I turned around to see a young man, wiping his face. He must have been walking past when I'd thrown the shot.

"Sorry." I grabbed him by the arm and led him a few feet down the bar, so he wouldn't give the game away. "Are you okay?"

"Yeah." He smiled. "Although, to be honest, I usually prefer to *drink* my shots."

"I'm really sorry."

"That's okay. I take it that it's your hen night." He gestured to the T-shirt. "Can I buy you a drink?"

"I'd rather you didn't. I'd only have to throw it away again."

"Fair enough." He laughed. "All the best for the wedding."

"Thanks."

***

When we'd finished at Bubbles, I would have gladly called it a day, but there was no chance of that. Deli led the parade of pink witches across the city centre to Mushroom, a new nightclub, which had opened only a few months earlier. It was so dark inside that I assumed they must actually be trying to cultivate said fungus.

While no one was looking, I took off the T-shirt and dropped it into a waste bin.

Unfortunately, I wasn't able to use the 'fake cocktail' trick this time because Deli insisted on buying the first round. Instead, I settled for something called Mushroom Fantasy. It was sludge coloured and tasted like vinegar, but apart from that, it was fantastic.

I'd forgotten just how bad the twins were at dancing. They would tell you that in the sup world they were the toast of the dancefloor, but here in the human world, they still looked like they were doing synchronised swimming, minus the water. Despite my best efforts to avoid the dancefloor, Deli had insisted we all join the twins.

Mad looked as though she was having about as much fun as I was.

"What time is it?" I shouted over the music.

"Almost one o'clock."

"What time does this place close?"

"Six, I think."

"Please tell me you're joking."

She wasn't.

Somehow, I managed to last almost thirty minutes on the dancefloor. By that time, I was parched. I needed a long, cold, non-alcoholic drink.

The queues at the bar were insane. All except for one till where the barman was standing around, waiting for his next customer. Before anyone else could beat me to it, I made a beeline for him.

"Orange cordial, please. A large one with lots of ice."

"Sorry, love. This till is for Mushroom Members only."

I glanced at the long queues further down the bar. "How much does membership cost?"

"Sorry, membership is closed."

"Please. Have mercy on me. I'm getting married next week."

"That's what they all say."

"I really am. Look!" I pointed to the T-shirt. The one that was no longer there.

"That's a nice dress, but I still can't serve you."

Cursing under my breath, I joined one of the other queues. While I was waiting to be served, I kept my eye on the members-only till, and quickly realised that something strange was going on. The barman never once asked to see a membership card. Instead, he either served the customer immediately, or sent them away as he'd done with me. How did he know which customers were members? He couldn't possibly have memorised the face of every member. And then it dawned on me. Everyone he served was a vampire. All other sups and humans were sent away.

Another millennium came and went before I was eventually served.

I downed half of the cold orange in one go, and was about to return to the fray when I noticed two vampires were at the so-called members-only till. It was none of my business, but it occurred to me that investigating what was going on would give me an excuse to postpone the torture of the dancefloor.

I found a quiet spot beyond the cloakrooms and made myself invisible. Back inside, I clambered, unnoticed, over the bar. By then, another three vampires were being served. The barman didn't even ask them what they wanted to drink. Instead, he bent down and opened what appeared to be a safe. Only it wasn't—it was a fridge full of bottles containing a dark red liquid. It didn't take a genius to guess what was in them.

What do you mean, it's just as well?

Back at the cloakroom, I reversed the 'invisible' spell, and made a phone call.

"Jill?" Daze sounded surprised to hear my voice. "Isn't it your hen night tonight?"

"Unfortunately, yes. I was hoping you might be able to give me Blaze's number."

"Sure. Is everything okay?"

"Fine, yeah. I have a tip-off for him."

"Right. Are you ready?"

"Fire away." I took down the number, and then gave Blaze a call.

When I got back to the dancefloor, I was surprised to find all of my party were seated at tables.

"How come you lot aren't dancing?"

"There's no room since that crowd arrived," Amber pointed.

The dancefloor was full of old wrinklies—all shaking their booties. Not a pretty sight, I can tell you. And then I saw her.

"Grandma?" I turned to Aunt Lucy. "What's she doing here?"

"Apparently, the bridge club finished early, so she persuaded them all to come here."

At that moment, the music stopped, and the main lights came on. There was lots of banging and shouting, and then several uniformed police officers burst through the doors.

The one who appeared to be in charge called for everyone's attention. "Ladies and gentlemen, I'm sorry to put an end to your fun, but I have to request that you all leave immediately."

To the sound of much moaning and groaning, the nightclub slowly emptied.

"Thanks for the tip-off, Jill," Blaze, dressed as a policeman, whispered as I walked past him.

Outside the club, Deli had gathered everyone together. Grandma and her cronies were there too.

"Don't panic," Deli said. "We'll go to Toadstool."

"What's Toadstool?" I said to Mad.

"It's another club. A bit like this one. It's a couple of miles out of town."

"I don't think I can take any more of this."

"Me neither."

Deli had taken charge of the taxis. Grandma and her entourage took the first three. The twins, Aunt Lucy and Deli climbed into the next one.

"Get in you two," Deli shouted. "There's plenty of room."

"It's okay. We'll take the next one and see you there."

When the taxi pulled away, I turned to Mad. "Pizza?"

"I fancy a burger."

"Okay. Burgers it is then."

Chapter 13

"What time is it?" Jack groaned when I climbed out of bed.

"Seven."

"Why are you getting up?"

"I have to go to the cat show, remember?"

"I feel like death." He looked like it too.

"It's your own fault. You must have really been putting it away last night."

"Could you speak a little quieter, please? My head is pounding." He rubbed his temple. "I only had three or four drinks."

"And the rest. When the taxi dropped you home, you were singing at the top of your voice."

"I wasn't. Was I?"

"Goodness knows what the neighbours will think. No one wants to be woken by the laughing policeman at four in the morning."

"What was I laughing at?"

"You weren't. That's what you were singing: The Laughing Policeman."

"I think I'm going to be sick." He jumped out of bed and rushed to the loo.

"Would you like me to make you a nice, greasy fry-up?" I shouted through the toilet door, on my way past.

Snigger.

After a couple of slices of toast and a cup of tea, I went upstairs to get showered and dressed. Jack was back in bed, doing his best impression of a corpse.

"Feeling any better, Dearest?"

"Not really. How come you're okay?"

"Because *I* didn't get drunk last night."

"I think I might stay in bed today." He rolled over.

"You have to do the weekly shop."

"Can't you do it?"

"I'm going to be at the cat show all day."

"Can't I just order it online?"

"There won't be any slots left for delivery today."

"I'll go later." He put the pillow over his head. "If I don't die first."

"Don't be such a wuss. It's only a hangover."

I'd often pondered what career I might pursue if I ever hung up my P.I. boots. It struck me that I'd make a good nurse, what with my empathy, compassion and bedside manner.

***

When I arrived at Kathy's house, Lizzie was watching for me through the front window. I was only half way up the drive when she opened the door.

"Mummy's poorly, Auntie Jill. Can we still go to the cat show? Please!"

"What's wrong with your mummy?"

"She's been sick. Daddy's not very well either."

Peter appeared in the doorway, looking as white as a sheet.

"Morning." He managed through dry lips.

"You look about as good as Jack."

"He got home okay, then?"

"Eventually. Where's Kathy?"

"In the lounge. Come on in."

If I'd thought Jack and Peter looked bad, that was nothing compared to Kathy who was lying on the sofa, feeling very sorry for herself. "I'm sorry, Jill. I'm not going to be able to make it."

"Can we still go, Auntie Jill?" Lizzie pleaded.

"Of course we can. Where's Mikey?"

"My mother is keeping him at her house until tonight," Peter said. "She brought Lizzie back because of the cat show."

"Right, Lizzie." I took her hand. "You go and get in the car while I say goodbye to your mummy and daddy."

"Okay!" She rushed out of the house.

"I'm really sorry, Jill," Kathy said.

"You owe me big time for this."

"I know. I'll make it up to you."

"You sure will."

As I left the house, Kathy was headed for the bathroom.

"What's the matter with mummy and daddy?" Lizzie asked, as we drove into Washbridge.

"It's probably just a bug. They'll be better by the time we get back."

***

As we climbed the stairs to my offices, a horrible thought struck me. What if Winky wasn't there? If he'd spent the night at one of his many lady friends', he could easily have forgotten about the cat show. What would I do then? Lizzie would be devastated.

I told her to wait in the outer office, just in case, but I needn't have worried. Not only was he there, but he was looking fabulous — there was no other word for it.

"So?" Winky did a twirl. "What do you think?"

"You've scrubbed up quite nicely. I've never seen you looking so — err — "

"Handsome?"

"I was going to say, clean."

"I called in at Molly's last night."

"Don't tell me she's yet another girlfriend?"

"No. She runs Molly's Feline Shampoo and Grooming."

"Well, I have to say, she's done an excellent job." I went over to the cupboard and took out the cat basket.

"Do I have to go in that thing?"

"They won't let you in otherwise."

He groaned a bit but climbed in anyway.

"Here's Winky," I held up the basket for Lizzie to see.

"I think he'll win, don't you, Auntie Jill?"

"I wouldn't get your hopes up."

"Of course I'll win," Winky chimed in.

"He's meowing a lot, isn't he, Auntie Jill?" Lizzie giggled. "It's like he knows what we're saying."

***

I'd assumed the cat show would be a small, local affair with about a dozen cats taking part.

Boy, was I wrong!

"Excuse me," I said to the woman standing in front of us in the queue. "Are there always so many people at these local shows?"

"It's not just the local show. The national finals are being held today too, didn't you know?"

"Err—no. How come they're being held in Washbridge?"

"They hold them at a different venue every year. It's Washbridge's turn."

Only then did I notice the basket at her feet. Inside it was a fluffy ball of something.

"Is that your cat?"

"Yes, Letitia is a two-time regional champion."

"Very nice." I gestured to my basket. "This is Winky."

She pulled a sour face. "What's wrong with his eye? Does he have fleas? He looks as though he might."

"No, he doesn't. He had a shampoo at Molly's only yesterday."

The woman muttered something under her breath, and then turned away.

"What's up with that stuck up cow?" Winky said.

"Shut up."

"Really!" The woman said. "There was no call for that."

"I wasn't talking to you. I was talking to—err—Winky."

She glared at me for the longest moment, and then turned away again.

When we eventually made it to the front of the queue, a surly man held out his hand for our tickets.

"Wrong queue."

"Sorry?"

"You're in the wrong queue. This queue is for the national final competitors only. You need the moggies' queue. It's down there."

"We've been queueing for twenty-minutes already. Couldn't you just turn a blind eye and let us in?"

"Sorry. You'll have to go down there."

I was worried that Lizzie might start to get restless, but fortunately there was one of her school friends in the moggies' queue.

"Oy!" Winky said. "What's with the two competitions?"

"One is for best of breeds that have won their way to the national finals. The other one is for—err—everyone else."

"I'm best of breed. I should be in that competition."

"What are you, anyway? I've often wondered."

"I'm a cat, of course. Jeez, you're even slower than I thought you were."

"No, I meant—err—never mind."

We eventually made it to the front of the moggies' queue where an officious man looked down his nose at me. "Take your cat through to Hall 'A', then you and the little girl will have to go through to the main hall."

"Can't we stay with our cat?"

He sighed. "I assume this is your first time at one of these shows?"

I nodded.

"The cats have to be put in cages for the judging. When the judges have finished, you'll be called through."

"Why can't we stay in there while they do the judging?"

He laughed. "You'd be surprised at the lengths some people will go to in order to influence the judges. This system ensures there's no opportunity for anything untoward."

We took Winky through to Hall 'A' and found the cage with his number on it. Lizzie's friend and her mother were just a few cages down, so while I transferred Winky from his basket, Lizzie went to see her friend's cat.

"Hey." Winky began to struggle in my arms. "I'm not going in that thing."

"You have to. Those are the rules."

"Nobody told me I'd have to be behind bars."

"I didn't know about it. Stop being so melodramatic. It's only until the judges have done their rounds."

"What do I win anyway? It had better be worth my while."

"I've no idea. Who says you're going to win?"

"Of course I'll win. Just look at the competition. Have you ever seen an uglier bunch?"

"Hi, I'm Elsie, Florence's Mum." Lizzie's friend's mother had come over to join me.

"Hi. I'm Jill."

"Where's Kathy?"

"She couldn't make it. She's—err—feeling a bit under the weather."

"The hen night?" She laughed.

"How did you know?"

"She mentioned it to me the other day. Wait a minute. You said your name was Jill, didn't you? Are you her sister?"

"That's me."

"Wasn't it *your* hen night? How come you managed to make it today?"

"I didn't really have a choice. I'd promised Lizzie."

"We're going through to the main hall to get a drink and a snack. Would you and Lizzie like to join us?"

"Sure, why not?"

"What about me?" Winky shouted after us.

I ignored him.

The muffins must have had small diamonds hidden inside them. It was the only thing that could have explained the ludicrous prices they were charging.

"How long does the judging normally take?" I said.

"When it's just the local show, it's usually no more than a half-hour, but because they're judging the nationals too, I suspect it'll be much longer. An hour and a half at least, I'd guess."

"Auntie Jill! Auntie Jill!" Lizzie came running up to me; she looked close to tears.

"What's wrong?"

"I forgot to put this on Winky." She had a red collar in her hand. "I bought it especially for him."

"Oh, well. Never mind."

"But this is a lucky collar. He won't win without it."

"I suppose I could nip back and—"

"They won't let you in," Elsie said. "Not until the judging has finished."

"Maybe they haven't started yet." I took the collar from Lizzie. "I'll go and see. Is it okay for Lizzie to stay here with you?"

"Of course."

I rushed back to Hall 'A' where I was confronted by Mr Jobsworth.

"I just need to put this collar on."

"I don't think it'll fit you." He chuckled at his own joke.

"Very funny. If I could just go back inside for a couple of minutes?"

"Sorry. No can do."

"Has the judging actually started?"

"Not yet, but any minute now."

"Well then. I'll be in and out in no time."

"Sorry. No entry until the judging has finished."

I was never going to talk my way past him, so I found a quiet spot, and made myself invisible. Then, as I slipped unseen by Mr Jobsworth, I accidentally kicked him on the shins.

Whoops.

Once out of sight of the entrance, I reversed the 'invisible' spell. I wasn't looking forward to seeing Winky. He'd no doubt be livid because we'd left him alone in 'prison'.

Boy, was I wrong.

"Winky? What's going on?"

"Hey guys, this is my two-legged." He stopped playing cards just long enough to introduce me to his fellow gamblers, but none of them seemed very interested in me.

"How did you all get out of your cages?"

"Those things?" He scoffed. "A two-week old kitten could get out of those."

"What about the judges? If they see you —"

"Chillax. Benny's keeping a lookout for them. What are you doing in here, anyway?"

"Lizzie wanted you to wear this lucky collar."

"Nice colour." He slipped it on. "You'd better make yourself scarce. We don't want the judges to think you're trying to bribe them."

"Okay. Good luck."

"I won't need it, but thanks."

I spotted a door through to Hall 'B', where the cats in the national competition were waiting to be judged, and I decided to take a quick look. The cats in there were much too busy preening and posing to start a card game.

I'd thought I was alone in the hall when I heard someone sneeze. And then sneeze again. Two men, wearing white coats, were standing close to the door at the opposite side of the hall.

"Stop sneezing!" the taller of the two said.

"I can't help it. I told you I was allergic to them."

Crouching below the cages, I made my way over to where the two men were standing. That's when I spotted the word printed on the back of their coats: Jugde.

Jugde? Seriously? If they couldn't even spell the word, how could they be qualified to judge anything?

"That's it! Over there!" The shorter man pointed.

"Right. The other man picked up one of the cages. "Let's go."

And with that, they disappeared out of the door.

I made myself invisible again, so I could get past Mr Jobsworth — giving him a kick on his other shin, on my way past.

"Did you do it, Auntie Jill?" Lizzie said.

"Yes. Winky looks really good in his new collar."

Five minutes later, an announcement came over the loudspeakers:

"Ladies and gentlemen, we apologise for the delay, but I'm sorry to report that Mr Sigmon has been stolen. If anyone sees him, please report it to one of the officials immediately."

"Who's Mr Sigmon?" I said to Elsie.

"He's the number one Persian in the country. He was the clear favourite to win today."

"Why would anyone want to steal him?"

"He's worth a small fortune."

"What's happening, Auntie Jill?" Lizzie said. "When will we know if Winky has won?"

"It won't be long. Elsie, I'm sorry to ask, but could you watch Lizzie again?"

"Of course."

'Jugde'? Those men were no more judges than I was, and I was pretty sure I knew what they'd been up to. I cast the 'listen' spell and waited. Sure enough, there was one sneeze followed by another. And then another.

I followed the sound to the indoor car park where I saw the men climb into an unmarked white Transit van.

I rushed over and pulled open the door. "I'll take those." I snatched the keys out of the ignition.

"What do you think you're doing?" the driver yelled.

"The next time you try something like this, I suggest you invest in a good dictionary."

"What are you talking about? Give me back those keys."

"I don't think so." I cast the 'tie up' spell, to bind them both hand and foot, then went in search of one of the security guards.

Back in the main hall, I re-joined Elsie and the girls just in time to hear the announcement:

"Ladies and gentlemen, I'm pleased to report that Mr Sigmon has been found safe and well. The judging will now proceed as planned. Another announcement will be made when the judges have finished, and you can return to the hall."

***

Late afternoon, when we arrived back at Kathy's, she and Peter were looking slightly less zombie-like.

"Winky won!" Lizzie screamed.

"That's fantastic, Pumpkin, but do you think you could speak a little quieter. Mummy has a headache."

"Look, Mummy!" Lizzie held up the certificate and rosette. "Can I put them on my bedroom wall?"

"Of course you can. Daddy will help you, won't you, Daddy?"

"Now?" Peter was obviously still feeling very fragile.

"Yes, please, Daddy." Lizzie grabbed his hand.

"Okay, then. Come on."

"I'm sorry about today, sis," Kathy said when we were alone.

"It's okay. It turned out to be more fun than I expected."

"I can't believe that ugly cat of yours won."

"Apparently, they judge the moggies mainly on character. The head judge said Winky had more personality than any cat she'd ever encountered. He got a certificate and rosette too."

"Are you going to stay for a drink?"

"No, thanks. I'd better get back to see how Jack of the walking dead is doing."

Chapter 14

Early on Monday morning, I had a phone call from Blaze who called to thank me for the tip-off. He confirmed that they'd closed down the human blood sales in Mushroom. Plus, as a result of information given up by the barman, who was trying to save his own skin, Blaze thought they were now much closer to finding the 'Mr Big' who was behind the blood distribution network.

"We must never get divorced," Jack said, over breakfast.

"We aren't even married yet."

"I know, but when we are, we must never get divorced. After yesterday's hangover, I can't go through another stag night."

"Don't expect any sympathy from me. You should take a leaf out of my book: Moderation in all things."

"Like blueberry muffins?"

"That's different."

"And custard creams?"

"I seem to recall we were discussing your hangover."

"I can't believe that one-eyed cat of yours won the show."

"That's what Kathy said."

"He didn't speak to the judges, did he?"

"Of course he didn't. I'm the only one who can hear him talk."

"It must be great being able to talk to animals. I've often wondered what they're thinking. Does Winky have many profound thoughts to share with you?"

"Not exactly. Most of the time, all he wants to talk about

is salmon and his girlfriends."

"Plural?"

"Oh, yes. There's Judy, Daisy and — err — what's the other one? Oh, yes, Trixie."

"Wow! Who would have thought it? Just think, this time next week, we'll be husband and wife. You'll be Mrs Maxwell."

"That reminds me. I'd better check that Mrs V has ordered my new sign. I'm hoping it's going to be installed while we're on honeymoon."

My phone rang; it was Aunt Lucy.

"Jill? Are you okay?"

"I'm fine, but *you* don't sound very good."

"I'm not. I would have called yesterday, but I didn't have the strength to pick up the phone."

"Have you had the flu?"

"No. I'm still recovering from the hangover to end all hangovers. It's my own fault. I'm calling because I seem to remember that you didn't make it to the second nightclub, so I wanted to check you were okay."

"*I'm* fine, but I think you should go back to bed."

"Don't worry, I intend to."

"I'm going around to Pearl's later, to see the two Lils."

"Thank goodness I'm not meant to be babysitting today. I don't think I'd be able to manage it. Say hello to the twins for me, would you?"

"I will. Now try to get some sleep."

***

I'd tried numerous times to get hold of Graham Hardy, the fourth member of the bowling party, but he wasn't picking up, and he hadn't responded to my voicemails.

It was time for the direct approach.

"Graham Hardy?" I door-stepped him as he left his house.

"Who are you?"

"Jill Gooder. I tried calling you, but—"

"I have nothing to say to the press."

"I'm not the press. I'm a private investigator."

"I have nothing to say to you either."

"Jack Maxwell said he thought you'd talk to me. He and I live together."

"Oh, right, sorry. I didn't realise who you were. I was just on my way to the shops."

"I'd only need a few minutes of your time."

"Sure, I can go to the shops anytime. I've got all the time in the world since I lost my job. Shall we go inside?"

We went through to the kitchen where he made us both a cup of tea.

"Sugar?"

"Yes, one and two-thirds spoonfuls, please."

He gave me a puzzled look, and then passed me the sugar bowl.

"Do you live here alone, Graham?"

"Yeah. The wife left me the day after WashChem made me redundant."

"Oh dear. I'm sorry."

He shrugged. "It had been coming for a long time; losing my job was the last straw for Irene. She's living with her sister now—the two of them deserve one another." He managed a weak, but unconvincing smile. "Did you know that I left the bowling alley early on

Tuesday night?"

"Yeah. Jack mentioned it. Can I ask why you had to leave?"

"My brother hasn't been well. I had a phone call to say he'd been taken into hospital."

"I'm sorry. Is he okay?"

"He's doing better now, thanks."

"Did you hear that Chris Jardine has been charged with Bill's murder?"

"Yes. I suppose it was only a matter of time before he found out about Bill and Sarah, but I never thought he'd do something like this."

"You knew about the affair, then?"

"I've known about it for a while. I saw Bill and Sarah together."

"Did you say anything to Chris?"

"No. It wasn't my place to interfere in his marriage."

"I've spoken to Chris since he was arrested. He maintains he had no idea that his wife was seeing Bill."

Graham shrugged.

"Don't you believe him?"

"It's not for me to say, but if I knew about it, I'd be surprised if Chris didn't."

We'd finished, and I was on my way out of the door.

"Thanks for your time and for the tea."

"No problem."

"Incidentally, which hospital is your brother in?"

"Washbridge General. Why?"

"No reason."

I called Jack.

"I've just spoken to Graham Hardy. It seems he knew that Sarah and Bill were having an affair. If he knew, there must be a chance that Chris did too."

"I didn't know anything about it."

"Yes, but then you are the world's least observant person."

"Thanks."

"Do you know Graham's brother?"

"I've never met him. Graham mentions him occasionally. From what I can make out, he hasn't been in the best of health for a while. I'm sorry, but I have to get going – I have a meeting with my boss in ten minutes. I'll see you tonight. Love you."

"Love you, too. See you later."

***

I'd promised to go to Pearl's house, to see the two Lils.

Amber answered the door. "We're in the kitchen. Come on through."

"Hiya, Jill." Pearl was just putting the kettle on. "Tea?"

"I've only just had one but go on then."

"I have custard creams."

"I would hope so too. Where are Lil and Lil?"

"In the lounge."

"Can I take a quick peep? I won't wake them."

"It's okay. They're not asleep."

Fastened into their baby seats, the two Lils were both gooing with joy, as they watched the show which had been put on for their benefit. A show that was being performed by a dozen or more soft toys, which had apparently come to life.

"Amber! Pearl! Have you got a minute?"

The twins came rushing through to the lounge.

"What's wrong?" Amber sounded panic-stricken. "Is my Lil okay?"

"They're both okay."

"You scared me to death," Pearl scolded me.

"Sorry, but I seem to recall you told Aunt Lucy that under no circumstances could she use magic to amuse the Lils."

"Oh, that," Pearl said, sheepishly.

"Yes, that. This looks to me like a case of do as I say, not as I do."

"They take such a lot of entertaining," Amber said.

"I'm sure they do. That's why Aunt Lucy is shattered by the time she hands them back each day."

"You won't tell her, will you?" Pearl said.

"No, I won't."

"Phew."

"Because you two are going to tell her."

"We can't. She'll kill us."

"I don't care. It's your own fault. You have to let her know that it's okay for her to use magic to entertain Lil and Lil when she needs to."

"Okay, okay." Amber sighed. "We'll tell her."

"Tomorrow."

"You can be so hard sometimes, Jill."

The Lils were still totally engrossed in the show, so the three of us went back through to the kitchen.

"Is that all I get?" I stared at the two custard creams.

"A couple is more than enough for anyone."

"I know, but you've only given me two."

"Two is a couple."

"In theory, maybe."

"No, not in theory. A couple equals two. Always." Pearl put the packet back in the cupboard.

She could be so mean.

"Have you two recovered from the hen night?"

"Just about."

"That's more than I can say for Aunt Lucy."

"We haven't heard from Mum since Saturday night."

"When she called me earlier, she sounded like death warmed up."

"It was Mad's mother that did for her," Amber grinned. "That woman is crazy. Which reminds me, where did you and Mad disappear to? When we got to Toadstool, there was no sign of either of you."

"Mad was feeling a bit off it, so I took her home."

"That's strange." Pearl grinned. "When we spoke to Mad yesterday, she said *you'd* been feeling ill, so she took *you* home."

"Busted." I laughed. "We'd both had enough."

"You oldies can't take the pace."

"Talking about oldies, did Grandma manage to stay the course?"

"And then some. They had to practically drag her and her crew off the dancefloor when it was time to close."

I finished the second custard cream, coughed, and gestured to the empty plate, but Pearl simply ignored me.

"What's happening about the self-order machines? Have you been in touch with the supplier?"

"Not exactly," Amber said.

"What does that mean?"

"The number they gave us doesn't exist."

"But you know where they're based, right?"

Pearl shook her head. "Ron, the guy who sold them to us, just came into the shop one day."

"How did you contact him to place the order?"

"We did all the paperwork there and then in the shop."

"Isn't there an address on the paperwork?"

"Yeah."

"Well then?"

"That doesn't exist either."

Oh boy.

***

I'd no sooner magicked myself back to Washbridge than my phone rang; it was Desdemona Nightowl.

"Jill, I thought you'd want to know that there's been another theft. I heard about it just over an hour ago."

"What's been taken this time?"

"A gold bracelet belonging to Christine Ridings."

"Where was it taken from?"

"The Nomad girls' dormitory again."

"I'll be honest with you, headmistress, so far, I haven't come up with any meaningful leads."

"I'm sure you're doing your best, but if this continues, I'll have to call in the Candlefield police. I'd rather avoid that if I possibly can."

"How would you feel about my going undercover in the Nomad dorm?"

"What do you mean by undercover?"

"If I posed as a pupil, I'd be able to witness the goings on in that dorm more closely."

"I don't think that will work."

"I could use magic to make myself appear to be the right age."

"I don't doubt that you could, but there's no way we'd be able to explain the sudden appearance of a new pupil. New starters are only allowed to join the school at the beginning of a new term. The thief would be bound to realise something funny was going on."

"Right. Better scrap that plan then."

"From what you've just said, Jill, it sounds like you think it was an inside job."

"It's certainly looking that way. Can you give me a few more days before you call in the police?"

"Of course, but please keep me posted."

"Will do."

As I walked back to my office building, I spotted a man who was wearing the same horrible jumper as Finn Waters had sported at The Sea's The Limit. A little further along the street, a woman was wearing an identical jumper. By the time I'd reached my offices, I'd counted ten more people wearing them.

"Look, Jill." Mrs V held up her version of the same jumper. "What do you think?"

"I think Grandma's app must be very popular."

"What makes you say that?"

"I've just seen loads of people wearing the very same jumper. They must have been at The Sea's The Limit, and used the app to download the pattern. What I don't understand is how everyone managed to knit them so quickly."

"They probably did what I did and used the wap to speed things up."

"Hold on a minute. I thought the wap—err—app just produced a pattern based on the garment you'd photographed."

"That's all the basic wap does, but the premium version actually knits the jumper for you."

Now it was all starting to make sense. Until then, I hadn't been able to work out why Grandma would invest time and money into producing something that was being given away for free. "How much does the premium version cost?"

"It's subscription based. It costs nine-ninety-nine per month. It's a bargain when you consider how much time it saves."

"And how exactly does it work?"

"Once you've used the basic wap to capture the pattern, you have to put the wool and knitting needles in a dark room, and then you click on the 'Knit Now' option."

"What happens then?"

"I'm not really sure. You have to leave the room, or it won't work."

"I bet."

"You wait outside the room for ten minutes, then when you go back, hey presto the jumper is all done. It's like magic."

"It most certainly is." I started to walk towards my office, but then remembered something. "Mrs V, did you manage to order the new sign?"

"I did, dear. At least, I think so."

"Aren't you sure?"

"Mr Song is a very strange man, isn't he? All the time I

was trying to have a conversation with him, he insisted on singing."

"I did warn you."

"It might be as well if you give him a call yourself, just to be on the safe side."

"I'll do that."

When I'd discovered that the only prizes at the cat show were certificates and rosettes, I thought Winky would do his nut, but he'd been as proud as punch. In fact, he'd already put his certificate and rosette up on the wall.

"Didn't I tell you I'd win?" he said.

"You did."

"And did you hear what the head judge said about me?"

"I did." He was going to be unbearable from now on.

"While I think about it, you weren't planning to work late tomorrow night, were you?"

"I don't think so. Why?"

"I'm having a lady friend over for dinner. I've asked her to come to see my rosette and certificate."

"Not your etchings, then?"

"Sorry?"

"It doesn't matter. Who's coming over?"

"Daisy. No, wait, it's Judy."

"Are you sure about that?"

He thought about it for a while. "No, I'm wrong. Judy couldn't make it tomorrow. It's Trixie. Definitely Trixie."

Unbelievable.

Just then, Kathy came charging into my office; she didn't look a happy bunny.

"I'm sorry to burst in on you, Jill, but if I'd stayed in the shop for another minute, I would probably have murdered your grandmother."

"What's she done now?"

"It's bad enough that she opened a bridal shop right next door to mine, but now she's ripping off every idea I come up with. Last week, we ran a twenty-per cent off promotion on wedding albums, so guess what?"

"She did the same?"

"She offered thirty per cent off them. It's not just that— she's stealing our ideas too. We've just introduced a new range of environmentally friendly confetti. It took me forever to source a supplier, and I spent ages putting together a window display to feature the new range. This morning, when I walked past her shop, guess what? She's got exactly the same confetti, front and centre of her window."

"That's despicable. No one likes a copy cobra."

"You mean, copycat."

"I think you'll find it's cobra."

From the sofa, Winky nodded his approval.

After Kathy had eventually calmed down and left, I called the sign company.

"It's A Sign. Sid Song, singing."

"Mr Song, hi, it's Jill. My PA, Mrs V, called the other day about getting my current sign replaced."

"You're the private investigator, aren't you?" he warbled.

"That's right."

"Change of name to Maxwell?"

"Correct."

"It's all in hand. It should be installed next week."

"That's great. Thanks."

Chapter 15

I adore breakfast.

I just thought I'd put that out there.

It's the meal which offers such a wide range of options. Everything from cereal to toast to a full fry-up. And yet, Jack chose to eat sawdust (AKA muesli) almost every day. Sometimes, I had serious doubts about that man.

"Penny for them," he said.

"I was wondering if I should be getting married to a man who voluntarily eats muesli for breakfast."

"It's good for you, unlike that thing in your hand."

"There's nothing wrong with a sausage cob."

"How many sausages are in there?"

"Just a couple."

"Is that an *actual* couple, as in *two*, or your version of a couple, as in as many as will fit in the cob?"

"You're only jealous." I took a huge bite.

He screwed up his face in mock disgust, but deep down, I knew he'd swap his sawdust for my sausage cob, in a heartbeat.

No chance, buddy.

"Only four days now until we get married," he said.

"Three, actually. Today's Tuesday."

"I know. Tuesday, Wednesday, Thursday and Friday. That's four days."

"You're not supposed to count today."

"Of course you are."

"Everyone knows you don't count today when you're calculating how many days there are to go until something happens."

"This *everyone* of whom you speak. Would that be the same *everyone* who thinks that a couple can be any number you choose it to be?"

"I can't help it if you don't understand the fundamentals of mathematics. Incidentally, I thought I might take a look around the bowling alley today. Do you happen to know if they have CCTV?"

"They definitely do. What are you hoping to learn from that?"

"I don't really know, but I figure it can't hurt to take a look at it."

***

The bowling alley didn't open until midday, which was just as well because I had a meeting with my accountant, Luther Stone, in the morning.

On the short walk from the car park to my offices, I encountered another six of the now infamous jumpers.

"I think I might be in trouble, Jill." Mrs V looked worried.

"What's wrong?"

"I think I might get sued."

"Who would want to sue you, Mrs V?"

"That Waters man."

"Finn Waters? Why would he sue you?"

"Look." She passed me a copy of The Bugle.

The headline read: Counterfeit gang traced back to Washbridge.

A quick skim of the article revealed that Finn Waters' solicitors were trying to track down the source of counterfeit jumpers based on Mr Waters' design. It seemed that all the counterfeits had been traced to Washbridge and the surrounding area.

"Do you think I'll go to prison, Jill?"

"Of course not."

"But I'm guilty as charged. I did copy his jumper."

"You only made one based on his design, didn't you?"

"Yes. Just the one."

"You've got nothing to worry about, then. There is someone who should be worried, though, and that's the person who created the app, which is responsible for these counterfeits."

"Your grandmother? Maybe you should warn her?"

"I don't think so. Something tells me she'll be okay. She always is."

Luther was due any minute, and I was still trying to find all the receipts and invoices, which he would no doubt ask for. Why he couldn't just do my books without those, I'd never know.

"Which do you think?" Winky was holding up what appeared to be two tablecloths.

"What are you talking about?"

"For my dinner date tonight. Which tablecloth do you think says, young, professional and sexy?"

"They're just tablecloths. It doesn't matter which one you use."

"That's where you're wrong. A tablecloth can say a lot about a cat."

So much for Jack's theory on the profound thoughts of animals.

"You're insane."

"Don't forget to stay clear of the office tonight. I'll be entertaining my lady friend."

"Can you remember which one?"

"Of course I can. It's — err — "

"Trixie."

"I knew that."

"Typical man. Now, if you don't mind I'm trying to prepare for a meeting with my accountant."

"Oh dear."

"What do you mean, *oh dear*?"

"You're so self-delusional that you can normally convince yourself that this business is viable, but when the accountant confronts you with the cold, hard figures, pop! That particular bubble is well and truly burst."

"Shut up and go back to your tablecloths."

As always, Luther was smouldering with sexual chemistry. Of course, now that I was practically a married woman, I barely noticed.

"Nerves beginning to jangle?" he said.

"I'm too busy to be nervous."

From under the sofa, I heard Winky chuckle, but I ignored him.

"Maria is really looking forward to the wedding. She made me buy a new suit."

"It'll be your turn next."

"I hope so, but that really depends on Maria."

"Have you asked her to marry you?"

"Not yet."

"What are you waiting for?"

"I'm scared she might say no."

"She won't, trust me."

"We'll see. Anyway, I suppose we should get down to business."

"Here are the receipts and invoices you wanted."

"There aren't many here."

"That's everything."

"I don't see any fuel receipts."

"They're in the car. Probably."

"We've discussed this before, Jill. I need proof of all your expenses to reduce your tax bill."

"Can't you just stick a figure in for them?"

He sighed. "It doesn't work like that. You'll need to let me have them next time."

"Okay. Will do. How are the books looking, generally?"

"Would you like the good news or the bad news?"

"The good. Definitely the good."

"There isn't any. You've made a loss for the third consecutive month."

"That's not possible."

"The figures don't lie. You're going to need to do something about this and fast."

"What do you suggest?"

"It comes down to one thing, really. You need more clients. More cases to bill."

"It feels like I'm already working to full capacity."

"That simply isn't reflected in your billing. Are you doing a lot of pro-bono work?"

"Occasionally."

"Maybe you should cut back on that. And you need to think about some kind of marketing campaign. Something that will bring in the punters. Do you know anyone in marketing?"

"I do as it happens."

Much as I liked Luther, his visits always left me feeling down in the dumps. Surely, just once he could tell me how well the business was doing? Was that too much to ask?

Unfortunately, I knew he was right; I did need to raise the profile of my business somehow. The thought of having to ask Grandma for help filled me with dread, but she had proven time and time again that no one knew marketing better than she did.

* * *

Deloris Shuttlebug was back from her short break, and she'd agreed to spare me a few minutes. She lived close to Candlefield Leisure Centre in a delightful house that was shaped rather like a pear.

"Thank you for seeing me, Mrs Shuttlebug."

"Come in, come in, and please call me Deloris. I'm always happy to talk about Cuthbert; he was a darling man, and I miss him terribly."

"You have a lovely house."

"Thank you, dear. Cuthbert designed it himself—he had a passion for pears."

"And exotic animals, I believe?"

"Yes, they were his first love." She laughed nervously. "Apart from me, I hope. Now, before we start, we must have a drink. I have tea and coffee, but I'm rather partial to hot chocolate myself."

"A hot chocolate would be nice. It's ages since I had one."

The hot chocolate was delicious. So too was the huge slice of chocolate brownie.

"Desdemona Nightowl told me about your late husband's interest in exotic creatures."

"Desdemona is such a dear. She was so very kind to me when Cuthbert passed away. Are you interested in exotic creatures too?"

"Not really, but I am trying to identify a particular creature that was found close to CASS. Ms Nightowl mentioned a manuscript?"

"It was his life's work. He was so disappointed when he couldn't find a publisher who was prepared to take a gamble on it. These days, it seems like they're only interested in books by celebrities. It's a crying shame. It covers hundreds of creatures, including pictures of most of them."

"Photos?"

"A few, but in most cases, they're illustrations that Cuthbert drew himself."

"He must have been multi-talented. Could I take a look at the book?"

"Why don't you take it away with you? That way you can study it at your leisure."

"Are you sure that's okay?"

"Absolutely. Cuthbert would be thrilled it's being put to some use rather than gathering dust in the attic." She stood up. "I'll go and get it for you now."

***

After magicking myself back to Washbridge, I put the manuscript in the boot of my car, and then drove to Wash

Bowl—Jack's second home. The place was practically deserted with only two lanes in use.

The man behind the counter looked a bit like a bowling ball, with his round face and huge nostrils.

"My name is Jill Gooder. I'm a private investigator."

"Sorry?"

"Is it always so noisy in here?"

"This is nothing. You should hear it when all the lanes are going."

"I said, I'm Jill Gooder. I'm a private investigator. Do you know Jack Maxwell?"

"Shirtz? Of course. He's one of our best customers."

"What did you call him?"

"Shirtz. On account of how many bowling shirts he has."

"Really? That's very interesting. Well, Shirtz and I are getting married on Saturday."

"Pleased to meet you. I'm Tommy." He offered his hand. "Are you thinking of taking up the sport?"

"Me? No. It's not really my scene, and besides, we already have enough bowling shirts in our house. No, the reason I'm here today, is Bill Mellor's murder."

"Terrible business. I was on duty the night he died. Bill was a fantastic bowler. He'd won the North of England Cup for the last three years in a row, and was favourite to win it again this year."

"Did you know the others who were bowling with Bill and Jack that night?"

"Chris Jardine pretty much keeps himself to himself. I know Graham Hardy, obviously, because he works here part-time."

"Oh? Doing what?"

"A bit of everything, really, but mainly helping with the machinery—maintenance, that sort of thing. In return, he gets free bowling and a bit of cash-in-hand. He's been struggling a bit since he lost his job. Graham's a mean bowler too. He's been runner-up to Bill in the North of England Cup for the last three years. Is it true what I heard—that Chris Jardine murdered Bill?"

"He's been charged with the murder, but we don't believe he did it. That's why I'm investigating, and why I'm here today. Jack said you had CCTV."

"Yeah, inside and out."

"Is there any chance of burning me a DVD of the footage from that night, so I can study it properly on my laptop?"

"Sure. Why don't you help yourself to a drink while I'm doing it?"

***

Now, whenever I arrived home, I had to do a quick scan of the street for clowns.

What? No, of course I wasn't afraid of them. I just— err—well, I just had better things to do than get caught up in conversation with someone wearing a red nose and ridiculously long shoes.

Fortunately, today, the street was a clown-free zone, but I did notice someone at the house next door to Breezy and Sneezy. A woman was struggling to carry something from her car, so being a good neighbour, I made my way over there to help.

"Do you need a hand?"

She looked up, and I could see now what she was

carrying: A large reel of cable.

"Thanks. That would be great. This is much heavier than I thought."

I grabbed one end, and between us, we easily got it into the house.

"Thanks, you're a life saver. I'm Pauline Maker."

"Jill. We live just across the road."

"Nice to meet you. Shawn was supposed to collect the cable, but he had to visit his mother."

"Shawn?"

"He's my husband."

"I live with Jack. We're getting married on Saturday."

"Really? Congratulations."

"Thanks."

"Have you met the clowns next door?" She blushed. "Oh dear. I hope you don't think I was being mean. They really are clowns."

"It's okay. I've already met Sneezy and Breezy."

"Would you like a cup of tea, Jill? It's the least I can do."

"Thanks. Maybe another time. I really should get going."

"Okay. Thanks again for the help."

"No problem."

Jack was already home.

"Hello, Gorgeous." He welcomed me with a kiss. "Had a good day?"

"Not bad, Shirtz." I grinned.

"Who told you?"

"Tommy at Wash Bowl. He burned me a copy of the CCTV from Tuesday night. I thought we could look at it together after dinner."

"Okay. Did I just see you across the road at the new neighbours' house?"

"Yeah. Their names are Pauline and Shawn. Hopefully these two turn out to be okay. We're overdue some *normal* neighbours, what with the clowns, the cosplayers and Mr Ivers."

After dinner, Jack and I sat at the kitchen table with the laptop, to watch the CCTV from the bowling alley.

"Tommy was really helpful today."

"He's a good guy."

"He told me that he'd paid for his holidays last year with the profit from your bowling shirt purchases."

"You're so funny."

"This is the view from the camera that covered your lane." I pointed to the screen. "There you are."

On screen were four figures: two standing on the far lane, two on the near one.

"Look at Bill, laughing," Jack said. "That was after I'd missed a spare in the first frame."

To ensure we didn't miss anything, we watched the recording at normal speed. It was pretty boring—not helped by the fact that Jack insisted on describing every shot in detail.

"Chris did well to make that spare. That was the turning point in the match."

"Really?" Yawn. "Where did Graham just disappear to?" I pointed to the screen.

Jack thought about it for a few seconds. "Oh yeah, I remember. The balls got stuck so Graham went around the back to clear them."

"Does that happen a lot?"

"More often than it should. The equipment at Wash Bowl is really old. They could do with getting it all replaced, but I doubt they can afford it. It's not so bad when Graham is with us because he can go and sort it out. Otherwise, we have to press the 'call' button and wait until someone gets around to doing it."

I restarted the recording, and after a few minutes, we saw Graham Hardy go over to the seats, and take his phone out of his jacket pocket. Moments later, he spoke to the others and then left.

"I assume that's when Graham told you he had to leave, to go and see his brother?"

"Yes."

When the on-screen match was over, I switched to the second CCTV recording, which covered the car park.

"That's us." Jack pointed at the image of three men walking into view.

"Look," I said. "Chris is giving Bill a cigarette."

The *Jack* on screen climbed into his car and drove away. Moments later, Bill and Chris went their separate ways. It was eerie to think that only a few minutes after that, Bill would be dead.

"It's so sad," Jack said. "Bill had been so happy when I left him. Did you spot anything on that footage?"

"No, but I think I'm going to give it another run through."

"I have an early start in the morning, so I'll have to leave you to it."

We kissed, and Jack went up to bed. I grabbed a couple (that's my version of a couple, obviously—snigger) of custard creams and a cup of tea, then settled down to view the footage again.

This time, I spotted a few things that warranted further investigation.

Chapter 16

The next morning, by the time I'd dragged myself downstairs, Jack had already left for work. The sausages were calling to me, but I had a wedding dress to get into on Saturday, so I ignored them, and settled for a bowl of cereal.

I was just about to sit at the kitchen table when I heard what sounded like a lorry in the street outside. Being naturally curious (no, not nosey), I went through to the lounge and opened the curtains. Pauline, whom I'd met for the first time the day before, and a man, whom I assumed was her husband, but whose name I'd already forgotten, were guiding the lorry onto their drive. Moments later, two men climbed out of the vehicle and began to unload their delivery. From what I could make out, it appeared to comprise of a number of steel panels of various sizes. I was intrigued (no, still not nosey), but I couldn't think of a good excuse to go over there and ask what they were up to.

By the time I left the house, the lorry had gone, and there was no sign of Pauline or her husband.

"Morning, Jill."

Oh bum! I'd been caught by the Ivers.

"Morning, Mr Ivers. I'm just on my way to work."

"Me too. The home-movie rental business won't run itself."

"I guess not. See you later, then."

"Did you know your brother-in-law has signed up with Have Ivers Got A Movie For You?"

"So I heard." Sucker.

"If he recommends a friend or family member, he and they both get a free month."

"Right." Who cares?

"Has he been in touch with you about it yet?"

"Err—no. Anyway, I'd better get—"

"You should have a word with him. Maybe he's forgotten."

"Yeah, okay. Bye, then." I dived into the car.

Sanctuary.

***

When I arrived at my offices, there was a note pinned to the outer door, which read:

There are no jumpers being made on these premises. None at all.

I tore it down and went inside.

"Phew." Mrs V sighed. "It's only you, Jill. I thought it might be the counterfeit squad."

"I'm not sure there is such a thing." I held up the scrap of paper. "I assume you stuck this to the door."

"I thought it might put them off the scent."

"Do you think maybe you're over-reacting a tad?"

"I don't want a criminal record. What would Armi think?"

"I've seen dozens of those jumpers around Washbridge. Even if the counterfeit squad was a thing, which it isn't. And even if they decided to prosecute someone, which is unlikely. The person they'll go after is Grandma. It certainly isn't you."

"I do hope you're right, Jill. I don't think I could survive for long on prison food."

"I give you my word. You have absolutely nothing to worry about."

Winky was on the sofa, looking particularly sorry for himself.

"Good morning, Winky."

"Not really."

"What's wrong?"

"I'd rather not talk about it."

"Okay."

"If you must know, my dinner date didn't go very well last night."

"What went wrong?"

"If you ask me, she made a mountain out of a molehill. It was a simple mistake that anyone could have made."

"I assume you're talking about Trixie?"

"No. Daisy."

"I thought it was Trixie who was coming over?"

"Therein lies the problem. I'd got it into my head that it was Trixie who was coming over for dinner, but it turned out to be Daisy. Halfway through the starter, I inadvertently called Daisy, Trixie."

"Oh dear."

"I managed to talk my way out of that one. I told her that Trixie was my cousin who I'd been talking to earlier."

"And she bought that?"

"Yeah, but then I made the mistake of leaving my phone on the table while I went to get the dessert out of the fridge. Judy chose that precise moment to call me. Daisy saw the name come up on screen, and she totally lost the plot. I mean, there was no call for what she did." He rubbed his head. "Have you ever tried to get jelly out of your fur?"

I couldn't answer because I was laughing too much.

I intended to pay another visit to the bowling alley, but as it didn't open until midday, I thought I'd spend an hour or so looking through the manuscript that Deloris Shuttlebug had kindly loaned to me. It was rather unimaginatively titled: Exotic Creatures of Candlefield.

"What's that you're reading?" Winky jumped onto my desk.

"I thought you were busy feeling sorry for yourself."

"There's no point in losing sleep over Daisy. I've still got Judy and Trixie. I'm more annoyed about the jelly. So, what is it you're reading?"

"It's a manuscript about the exotic creatures that live in Candlefield."

"What's that ugly looking thing?" He pointed to the open page.

"It's a pouchfeeder. I had a run-in with one of those some time ago."

"Rather you than me. Why the sudden interest in exotic creatures? Aren't I exotic enough for you?"

"I'm trying to identify one in particular."

Just then, Winky's phone rang.

"Hi, babe. Of course I've missed you." He jumped off my desk and disappeared under the sofa, to continue his conversation. For his sake, I hoped he didn't get the names mixed up again.

The variety of creatures featured in the book was truly astounding. There were a few that I recognised: the scarlet horned dragon, for example. Some of them were terrifying; others, like the marmadellow, were unbearably cute. Cuthbert Shuttlebug had not only spent years on research, he'd also produced fabulous illustrations for the majority of creatures. The man had obviously been an accomplished artist.

And then I saw it: the aurochilla.

The illustration certainly resembled Fluff, and the accompanying text confirmed it.

Excited, I called Desdemona Nightowl.

"Headmistress, it's Jill."

"You sound very upbeat. Does that mean you have good news for me?"

"I think so."

"Who is the thief? Please tell me that it isn't one of the pupils."

"I can put your mind at ease on that score."

"Thank goodness. Who is it, then?"

"Would it be possible to come over and see you later today? I can fill you in then."

"Of course. How about this afternoon?"

"That'll be fine. Could we meet in the Nomad girls' dorm?"

"I don't see why not."

"Can you ensure that everyone who has had anything stolen is there?"

"I'm sure that can be arranged."

"Oh, and headmistress, could you make sure Felicity Charming is there too?"

"Err—yes, I suppose so."

"Great. See you later."

Winky had finished on the phone and was looking

much happier with life.

"Did you manage to remember her name this time?" I said.

"You know what they say about sarcasm, don't you?"

"That it's the highest form of wit?"

"You clearly think so. That was Judy. She invited me to go away with her this weekend."

"Lucky you."

"I had to tell her no, but she understood when I explained that I'd promised to be your pagecat."

"Don't worry your head about that. You should go with Judy."

"Certainly not. I couldn't let you down. My word is my bond. I promised to be there for your special day, and there I'll be."

Oh bum! Now I felt really bad.

***

Tommy wasn't behind the counter in Wash Bowl today. Instead, a tall, slim young man, with curly hair and a beard, was talking on his phone while picking his teeth. Who said the young couldn't multi-task?

"What size?" he said when he noticed me.

"Sorry?"

"What size shoes do you want?"

"I'm not here to bowl."

"I can't give you change for the vending machines."

"I don't need change. I'd like a word with Tommy."

"It's his day off. Gone t'zoo."

"*Gontzoo?*"

He sighed. I was clearly testing his patience. "He's gone

t'zoo. Took his nipper to see giraffes and stuff."

"The zoo? Right. Look, I spoke to Tommy yesterday about—"

"Sorry, babe, I've got to go," he said into the phone, and then in a hushed voice. "There's some weird woman here doing my nut in."

"I'm very sorry to be *doing your nut in*, but I'd like to take a look backstage at the machinery."

"Who are you, anyway?"

"I'm a private investigator. I spoke to Tommy yesterday."

"He didn't say anything to me about no private investor."

"*Investigator*. Can you give him a call?"

"He's gone t'zoo."

"So?"

"If his phone rings, it might frighten the giraffes."

"I just need a quick look around the back at the machinery that operates the skittles."

"Pins. They're called pins."

"Whatever. Can I take a quick look?"

"No. H and S."

"What?"

"Health and Safety. Only staff allowed back there."

"You can accompany me."

"I can't leave this desk."

"Is there anyone else on duty?"

"Just me. Tommy's—"

"Gone t'zoo. Yeah, I know. Never mind."

I was getting nowhere fast, so I found a quiet corner and made myself invisible.

Fortunately, the door to the machine room was

unlocked. Once I was inside, I had to try to figure out which set of machinery belonged to the lanes where Jack and the others had been playing. I was still trying to work it out when a huge crash made me almost jump out of my skin. It took me a few seconds to realise that it was the sound of a bowling ball hitting the pins. Although it had scared me to death, it proved to be very helpful because I remembered that the only lane in use was the one three down from where Jack had played.

Having located the correct lane, I began to dig around. Jack had said the machinery at Wash Bowl was old, and he hadn't been kidding. There was dust, grime and all manner of creepy crawlies back there. I was just beginning to think that my hunch had been wrong when I noticed that one of the small metal grilles was being held in place by only a single screw. I slid the grille to one side and poked my hand inside. It was even more gross in there, but then my fingers brushed against something. I had to practically dislocate my shoulder to get a grip on it, but I finally managed to pull it out.

***

As arranged, the headmistress was waiting for me outside the Nomad girls' dorm.

"The others are inside, Jill."

"Felicity too?"

"Yes, although I should warn you she's a little tearful today. Have you seen that strange little creature of hers?"

"Fluff? Yes, he's awfully cute."

"That's as maybe, but I'm afraid Felicity is going to have to release him at the end of the week. The school doesn't allow unidentified creatures to be kept as pets."

"Shall we?" I held open the door.

Seated around the table were Beth Nightling, Felicity Charming and three other girls I didn't know. Felicity's eyes were red from crying.

"The floor is yours, Miss Gooder." The headmistress took a seat at the head of the table.

"Thank you, headmistress. Before I reveal who took the gold jewellery, I have some important news for Felicity. I'm pleased to report that I've managed to identify Fluff."

"Really, Miss?" Her eyes lit up.

From my pocket, I produced the photocopy I'd taken of the page from Cuthbert Shuttlebug's book. "Fluff is an aurochilla." I pointed to the illustration.

"Does that mean I can keep him, headmistress?" Felicity said.

"I suppose so. That illustration does appear to be your little friend, so I see no reason why you can't."

"Which brings me to the matter of the gold jewellery that has gone missing." I walked over to Fluff's cage and carried it across to the table.

Everyone, including the headmistress, looked confused.

"I brought this with me." I took a small earring out of my pocket. "I lost the matching one years ago, but I didn't throw it away because it's gold."

They now looked even more confused.

"Watch." I put the earring through the bars of Fluff's cage.

The cute little creature grabbed it, stuffed it into his mouth and began to eat it. A few moments later, it had gone, and he gave a tiny burp.

"The aurochilla are friendly creatures. They're very

rare – almost extinct, in fact. One peculiarity about them is that, as well as their normal diet of fruit and veg, they enjoy nothing better than eating gold."

Everyone looked stunned; no one more so than the headmistress. "How can a little thing like that manage to chew its way through gold?"

"According to Cuthbert Shuttlebug's notes, the aurochilla has a second set of incredibly strong teeth, which are hidden most of the time. It uses them to bite and chew gold."

"Fluff ate my ring?" Beth looked gobsmacked.

"And my bracelet?" said the girl who I now realised must be Christine Ridings.

"That's right. What's more, I believe he also ate the inter-house sports cup. Felicity has been having some problems with the catch on the cage. My guess is that Fluff managed to sneak out one night and had a really big feast on the trophy."

There was silence for the longest moment, but then the headmistress laughed out loud. "Well, blow me down. Whoever would have guessed? Still, I'd much rather it was this little creature than have a thief in our midst. I guess we'll just have to find the funds from somewhere to buy a replacement cup."

"That may not be necessary, headmistress." I turned to Felicity. "Could I have a quiet word?"

"Of course, Miss."

I took her to one side and told her what I wanted her to do.

She nodded, giggled and then picked up Fluff's cage.

"Would you come with us, please, headmistress?" I said.

Ms Nightowl looked very puzzled but followed as Felicity led the way out of the building.

"I usually take him over there." She pointed to a small copse in the distance, close to the perimeter wall.

"Lead the way."

The three of us made our way across the playing fields, which had already been marked out in preparation for Friday's sports day. When we reached the copse, Felicity stopped and looked at me.

"It's okay." I nodded. "Let him out."

She placed the cage on the ground, pulled the catch, and opened the door. Fluff didn't need any further invitation. He skipped out of the cage and scuttled into the trees.

We followed at a distance until we saw him stop.

"Wait here a minute," I said.

When he turned around and came back, Felicity put him in the cage, then I led the way to the spot where he'd halted for a while.

"Look!" I pointed.

"Is that what I think it is?" The headmistress pulled a face.

"Yes, it is. It's solid gold poo. I'm pretty sure there'll be lots more of it around here. It may not look very pretty, but once it's been cleaned up, it should still retain much of its value. If you collect it, there should be more than enough to pay for a new trophy."

"I'll get Reginald Crowe straight on it."

Poor old Reggie.

"Miss," Felicity said. "I don't think I want to keep Fluff."

"Why not? It's okay now we've identified him. You'll just have to keep him away from the gold."

"I was thinking about what you said about them being almost extinct. He probably has a family or friends back at the Valley of Shadows. I'd like to take him back there and set him free."

"That's a very selfless thing to do. What do you think, headmistress? Could that be arranged?"

"Absolutely. I'll get straight onto it as soon as I get back to my office."

"Great. I suppose I'd better get back to Candlefield, then."

"Before you go, Jill. I'd like to ask your permission to name the replacement inter-house sports trophy, the Gooder Cup."

"I'm very flattered, but that really isn't necessary. Anyway, my name won't be Gooder after Saturday."

"All the more reason to give your current name to the cup. It will act as a permanent reminder of when Candlefield's most powerful witch first taught at our school. What do you say?"

"I — err — guess so. Thank you very much."

"Excellent. In that case, you really must be here on Friday to present it to the victorious house."

"But, headmistress, I — "

"I realise you get married the next day, and will have a lot on your mind, but if you could just see your way clear to being here for the final event of the day: The final of the mixed four-hundred metres relay. You could present the trophy immediately after that race, and then shoot off home. What do you say?"

"Please say yes, Miss," Felicity said.

"How can I say no? I'll be here."

Chapter 17

It had been ages since I'd had breakfast at Aunt Lucy's, but then, yesterday, when I'd just happened to mention that Jack would have to go into work early today, she'd suggested I should join her this morning.

What? No, of course I hadn't been angling for an invitation. What kind of person would do that? Sheesh!

"Morning, Jill." Aunt Lucy was in the lounge, cradling one of the Lils in her arms.

"Morning. Which one is that?"

"Lil One." She hesitated. "Oh dear. I really shouldn't call her that, but it's the only way I can keep track of them. This is Amber's Lil."

"Lil One and Lil Two?" I like it. "I'm not sure Pearl would be very happy to know her little darling is number two, though."

"She'd be mortified, even if I tried to explain it doesn't mean anything. You won't tell either of them, will you?"

"Of course not. Your secret is safe with me."

"Take her, Jill, would you?" She handed Lil One to me. "Watch her while I see to breakfast."

"Me? I don't know how."

"You'll be fine. I won't be long."

"Err—okay."

Lil One seemed to be giving me a puzzled look. She could probably sense that I didn't have the first clue about babies.

"Goo, goo, goo," I said.

Lil One appeared to smile, so I was obviously on the right track. This looking after babies was a piece of cake.

"Goo, goo, goo."

She suddenly began to wail.

Oh no! What had I done?

"Aunt Lucy! Help!"

Moments later, she appeared at the door. "Did you call?"

"I think I've done something wrong. Lil One's crying."

"That's what babies do." Aunt Lucy smiled. "It's nothing to worry about. Just rock her in your arms and talk to her."

"I *was* talking to her. I said, 'goo, goo, goo', but that just made her cry."

"Try talking to her properly—just like you would to anyone else."

"But she's just a baby. What shall I talk to her about?"

"Tell her about the wedding."

"Seriously?"

"Why not? I'd better get back and see to the bacon."

"Hey, Lil, I'm getting married on Saturday. To Jack. You don't know him, but I think you'd like him."

To my amazement, Lil One stopped crying.

"I've got a lovely dress, and we're going to have a big cake. There's going to be lots of—"

I stopped because Lil One was fast asleep.

When Aunt Lucy returned, I whispered, "I think she must have been bored by all the wedding talk."

"She's due a nap. Pass her to me, and I'll put her down in the bedroom."

No one did a fry-up like Aunt Lucy.

"Will Lil be okay in there by herself?" I said.

"She'll be fine. If she stirs, I'll hear her on that." She

pointed to the small intercom.

"I've never been very good with babies," I said.

"Neither were the twins until the Lils came along. You'll be fine too when your turn comes, and you'll always have me to babysit."

"Thanks, but by that time, the Lils will probably be old enough to babysit for me."

"We'll see. It might happen sooner than you think. Oh, by the way, the twins came over the other night. They said that if I needed to use magic to amuse the Lils, they wouldn't have any objections. I'm not sure what prompted that sudden change of heart."

"Me neither." I grinned.

"You know something about it, don't you?"

"I might, but I'm sworn to secrecy."

"Go on. You can tell me."

"Okay, seeing as how you've twisted my arm. When I went to Pearl's house on Monday, the twins had used magic to get the soft toys to put on a show for the Lils. I told them that they had to own up, and let you know that you could do the same."

"The cheeky little madams! Just wait until I see them again."

Snigger.

I soaked up the last of the tomato juice with a piece of fried bread, and then popped it into my mouth. "That was delicious, Aunt Lucy. Thanks very much."

"My pleasure. I don't suppose I'll see you again before the wedding."

"Probably not."

"I'm really looking forward to it. So is your

grandmother."

"Really? I didn't think she approved of me marrying a human."

"She likes to pretend that she doesn't, but I can tell she's thrilled for you both. She just hides it well."

"Extremely well. I suppose I'd better get going."

"Could you do me a favour, Jill?"

"Of course."

"Amber left her purse here when she dropped Lil One off this morning. Is there any chance you could nip into Cuppy C and let her have it?"

"No problem."

When I arrived at the tea room, Amber was just tearing a slip from the terminal. "Chicken nuggets and a chocolate milkshake."

"Coming up." Mindy was standing next to the coffee machine.

"Since when have you sold nuggets?" I said.

"Chicken nuggets equals a latte." Amber pointed to the slip. "And the chocolate milkshake is a strawberry cupcake."

"Say what?"

"We've cross-referenced the items on the Burger Bay menu to the items on our menu. That way we can still use the self-order machines."

"Isn't it all a bit confusing?"

"It was at first, but we've just about got used to it now, haven't we, Mindy?"

"Yeah. Pretty much."

"So, you're keeping the machines?"

"We might as well, seeing as we've paid for them. Did

you want a hotdog?"

"What's that?"

"A blueberry muffin."

"No, thanks. I just popped in to bring you this. You left it at Aunt Lucy's."

"Thanks. I'd forget my head if it was loose. How's Lily?"

"When did you start calling her *Lily*?"

"William and I had a long talk last night. It's silly that both babies are known by the same name. It might confuse them when they're older, so we've decided that we're going to start calling Lil by her full name: Lily."

"That makes sense." Those are not words I often said to either of the twins. "Have you told Aunt Lucy?"

"No. I forgot to mention it when I dropped her off this morning, but I will do when I pick her up tonight."

Just then, I spotted a newspaper that someone had left on one of the tables. It was the headline that caught my eye: *Return of the Gold Gobbler*.

Amber noticed me reading the article. "Did you know about that?"

"I did, but I'd really love to know how The Candle got hold of the story. The creature was only identified yesterday."

"Is it true that it eats and poos gold?"

"Yeah, it does. It's really cute though."

Once I was outside Cuppy C, I made a call to Desdemona Nightowl.

"Have you seen The Candle, headmistress?"

"I have."

"How did they get hold of the story so quickly?"

"I don't know, but I suppose any of the staff or pupils could have tipped them off."

"I thought I'd better warn you because there's likely to be more press interest in this story."

"I'm way ahead of you, Jill. They'll no doubt be over here in their droves later today. That's why I've arranged for the little creature to be taken back to the Valley of Shadows immediately. By the time the press arrives on the airship, they'll be too late."

***

I'd called Graham Hardy, and he'd said I could pay him another visit.

We were in the lounge at his house.

"Thanks for agreeing to see me again, Graham."

"No problem. I'm surprised you're still working, though. Don't you and Jack get married on Saturday?"

"We do, yes, but I'm hoping to wrap up a few loose ends before then."

"From what I hear, it isn't looking good for Chris."

"He's an innocent man, so he has nothing to worry about." I glanced around. "Jack tells me you've won a lot of tournaments. I'm surprised you don't have any trophies on display."

"They're in the dining room. Would you like to see them?"

"Yes, please."

He led the way into the next room where a large glass cabinet had pride of place on the far wall.

"That's quite a collection." I feigned interest in the many cups.

"Thanks. I like to think so."

"No North of England trophy, though?"

"Not yet."

"I believe you've been runner-up to Bill Mellor for the last three years?"

He nodded. "I've just had a run of bad luck."

"Was it really worth killing him, just so you could win this year?"

His expression quickly changed to shock and then to anger.

"What are you suggesting?"

"I'm not *suggesting* anything. I'm *saying* you murdered Bill Mellor and framed Chris Jardine—all to give yourself a better chance of winning the North of England competition."

"That's absolute nonsense. Chris killed Bill because he was seeing Sarah."

"Chris knew nothing about his wife's affair."

"He would say that, wouldn't he?" Hardy pointed to the door. "I'd like you to go now."

"You almost got away with it, but then you'd been planning this for quite some time, hadn't you?"

"I don't know what you're talking about. If you don't leave, I'll—"

"Do what? Call the police? Go ahead. It'll save me the trouble of doing it."

"Chris poisoned Bill with a cigarette. The police have already confirmed that."

"But you and I know that isn't true, don't we, Graham? The poison that killed Bill got onto his fingers from the bowling ball, not from a cigarette."

I could tell by the look of terror in his eyes that he knew

the game was up, so I continued, "I found the glove you wore when you put the poison into the fingerholes of Bill's ball. As soon as he'd played his next shot, you took your imaginary phone call, made your excuses and left. No one noticed that you'd taken Bill's ball instead of your own. Why would they? They're identical. My guess is you went straight from the bowling alley to Bill's house, where you dropped the cigarette butt that you'd coated in the same poison."

"That trophy should have been mine. My average score has been better than Bill's for the last three years, and yet every time that competition comes around, he gets lucky."

"Was it really worth killing him just for a trophy?"

He didn't answer, but then he'd already proven that he thought so.

Susan Shay and her merry men turned up an hour later. I intercepted her at the door.

"This had better be good, Gooder."

"You'll have to come up with another line after Saturday."

"What are you talking about?"

"The *good, Gooder* line won't work after I'm married."

"I heard you and Jack were getting hitched. I'm disappointed in him—I thought he had more sense and higher standards."

"We sent you an invitation, but you didn't RSVP."

"I never received— oh, right, another one of your jokes. Where's Hardy?"

"In the dining room."

"If this turns out to be a wild goose chase, I'll take great pleasure in charging you with wasting police time. We already have enough evidence to convict Jardine."

"Luckily for you, I'm about to stop you sending an innocent man to prison. Hardy is ready to give you a full confession."

"We'll see. Don't go anywhere because we're going to need to talk to you too."

"My pleasure, as always, Susan."

***

There was nothing I enjoyed more than having to wait around Washbridge police station. I'd been left to twiddle my thumbs in a cold interview room all day, and I'd have bet good money that it was Sushi who had turned the heating off.

When I was eventually allowed to leave, there was no sign of Sushi, and certainly no apology or thanks. Instead, she sent a uniformed officer to see me.

"Jill? I'm Steve Pickering. Jack and I worked together a few times. Isn't it this Saturday that you and he get hitched?"

"It's supposed to be, but at this rate, I may still be here on Saturday."

"I'm really sorry about all this. I can't understand why you've been kept here so long."

I could.

"It's not your fault, Steve. Do you know what's happened with Hardy?"

"I shouldn't really be telling you this, but he's already been charged with Bill Mellor's murder."

"And Chris Jardine?"

"I imagine he'll be released before the night's out."

***

I arrived home just a few minutes before Jack.

"I've been trying to call you all afternoon," he said when he walked through the door.

"Sorry. I've been stuck in Washbridge police station all day, courtesy of Sushi. I couldn't get a signal in there."

"Are you okay?"

"I'm fine, but Sushi is definitely off my Christmas card list."

"You should register a formal complaint."

"It's not worth it, and besides, I'm used to dealing with difficult police officers."

He smiled. "A little bird told me that Graham Hardy has confessed to Bill's murder, and that Chris is going to be released. I assume you had something to do with that?"

"Look, I'm starving. Why don't we order in pizza, and I'll tell you all about it?"

"Sounds like a plan."

One Minute Takeaway failed to live up to their very high standards, and we had to wait almost *ninety seconds* for our pizzas to be delivered.

What was the world coming to?

Jack and I sat at the kitchen table, with my laptop.

"This is it." I pointed to the screen, which was displaying the CCTV footage from the bowling alley. "See, that's Graham's ball. And there, the ball that comes back up the chute is Bill's."

"What does it matter? They're identical."

"It matters because when Graham went around the back to the machine room, he put poison in the fingerholes of Bill's ball. Then he waited until Bill had played his next two shots, and then pretended to take a phone call."

"How do you know he didn't actually get a call? Have you checked his phone records?"

"I didn't need to. Just watch him. He's standing near the carousel watching the balls, and then he suddenly hurries over to his jacket and takes out his phone." I paused the footage.

"So?"

"The noise in that bowling alley is unbelievable when all the lanes are in use. There's no way he would have heard his phone ring above all that din."

"You couldn't know that for sure."

"True, but it was the first hint that something wasn't quite right. Watch him now." I restarted the footage. "Did you see which ball he picked up?"

"That was the one which Bill had just played with."

"Exactly."

"He could have just got them mixed up. He was probably stressed after the phone call about his brother."

"The phone call that never happened?"

"But his brother *has* been ill."

"That's the one part of his story that is true. His brother was taken into hospital, but that was two days earlier."

"You checked?"

"Of course."

"So, if I understand you correctly, Graham put the poison in the fingerholes of Bill's ball when he went in the machine room to free the trapped balls?"

"That's right. Having worked at a chemical factory for as long as Graham had, I don't imagine he found it difficult to find a poison that would do the job. I found the glove he'd worn, hidden behind a grille in the machine room."

"What I don't get is how Graham knew that he'd have the opportunity to apply the poison. He couldn't know the balls would get stuck."

"Whose idea was it to play this series of games between the four of you?"

"Err—Graham's, I think."

"I thought as much. He played the odds. He couldn't be sure when the balls would get stuck, but it was a pretty safe bet that it would happen at some time over a series of five matches. He just had to have enough patience to wait until it did."

"What about the cigarette butt?"

"Graham had been quietly fuming about Bill for years. He couldn't bear the thought of losing out to him again in the North of England competition. When he discovered that Bill was seeing Sarah, he saw an opportunity to get rid of him, and to frame someone else for the murder. He put traces of the same poison on the cigarette butt, and dropped it outside Bill Mellor's house, where he knew it would be found by the police."

"He might have got away with it too if it wasn't for my very own intrepid private investigator."

"My bill will be in the post."

"Do you take payment-in-kind?"

"Depends what you had in mind."

"When we've finished this pizza, I'll show you."

Chapter 18

"I can't believe we're getting married tomorrow." Jack had forsaken his beloved muesli in favour of an oat and sultana bar.

"We aren't. You must have had a nightmare."

"Spending the rest of our lives together isn't a nightmare. It's a dream come true."

"Aren't you sweet? If you didn't have a mouthful of oats and sultanas, I'd give you a kiss."

"Don't forget we have to be at the hotel at ten this morning, to run through the final arrangements with Marceau."

"Why do you need me there? You and Marceau have done fine without me until now."

"This is our last chance to make sure everything is okay. We should both be there."

"Okay, but I need to drop into the office first. I'll meet you at the hotel at eleven."

"Ten."

"That's what I said. Ten."

***

"Jill?" Mrs V looked up from her knitting. "I wasn't expecting to see you this morning. Shouldn't you be getting ready for tomorrow?"

"I've only popped in for a while. I'm meeting Jack and the wedding planner at the hotel at ten. How come you're knitting by hand? Has the app stopped working?"

"I'm done with that new-fangled technology. I told Armi he could have my phone. I've managed all these years without one—I can live the few I have left without one too."

"Any messages for me?"

"Yes, actually. A Mr Christopher Jardine called. I told him that you wouldn't be in for a couple of weeks. He said to tell you thank you for saving him. He seemed to think you'd know what he meant."

"I do, thanks. Anything else?"

"No, just that."

"What do you think?" Winky said. "Blue or green?" He held up first one bow tie and then another.

"Err—blue. Why have you got your tux on today?"

"Just a dress rehearsal. I want to make sure everything is perfect for your big day. I don't want to let you down."

Oh bum! As if I didn't already feel bad enough. Maybe I should have just come clean and told him where the wedding was actually taking place. But how could I? What on earth would people think if they saw a cat, wearing a tux, walking down the aisle behind me?

I was busy trying to make sense of this month's accounts when Mrs V came through to my office.

"You haven't forgotten you're supposed to be going to the hotel, have you?"

"Of course not. I don't need to be there until—oh bum— is it really that time?" I grabbed my bag and bolted for the door. "See you tomorrow."

***

We were in the Crimson Room at Washbridge Park

Hotel. It had been set out ready for our reception, which would take place in just over twenty-four hours' time.

Say what you like about Marceau, but the guy knew how to organise a wedding. Nothing had been left to chance. Even so, by midday, my patience was wearing thin.

"Are we nearly done?" I sighed.

"Yes, that about wraps it up." Marceau stood up.

"I'll walk Marceau back to his car," Jack said.

"Okay. I'll see you back home."

"You can't leave just yet. The cake is being delivered in twenty minutes time. We need to wait until it's arrived."

"Can't Marceau wait here for it?"

"He has to go and see the limousine people to check everything's okay with them. It's only a few more minutes."

"Okay, but I'm starving."

"Don't eat the cake if it comes before I get back."

"You're so funny."

Jack and Marceau had no sooner left than a young man came through the door.

"I'm a little early. I have a cake in the van for Gooder and Maxwell."

"I'm Jill Gooder. Would you bring it in here, please?"

"Will do."

So far, I'd only seen a photograph of the cake when Jack and I had chosen it from the glossy brochure. Jack had wanted the smaller one with three tiers, but I'd insisted on four. It was my wedding, and I planned on eating a lot of cake.

A few minutes later, I heard someone outside the door. I

assumed it must be the young man, back again. It sounded as though he was struggling, so I hurried over, and pulled the door open.

Whoops!

He must have been leaning against the door, trying to push it, because when I pulled it open, he fell into the room, spilling the bottom tier of the cake onto the floor.

What a mess!

"I'm so sorry." He looked like he might burst into tears. "I didn't know you were going to open the door."

Before I could say anything, Jack walked in.

"What happened?" He stared at the cake that was now splattered across the floor.

"I'm really sorry," the young man stuttered.

"It's okay," I said. "It wasn't your fault."

"What are we going to do?" Jack looked horrified. "We'll never get another one in time for tomorrow."

"I can sort this out." I looked at Jack. "But I'm going to need your permission."

"Permission to do what?" And then I saw in his eyes that the penny had dropped. "Oh, right. Yeah, okay, do it."

I cast the 'take it back' spell, and the cake was as good as new again.

"What the−?" The delivery man stared in disbelief at the cake.

I quickly cast the 'forget' spell on him.

"Can you bring the rest of the cake in from the van, please?"

He looked somewhat disorientated but managed to head back outside.

"Thank goodness you're a witch." Jack grinned.

"Shush! Not so loud."

"How come he didn't remember what had just happened?"

"I cast a spell that made him forget."

Jack seemed to consider that for a few moments. "Have you ever done that with me?"

"What?"

"Cast a spell to make me forget things?"

"I forget."

"Jill! Have you?"

"Yes, a few times, but only when you stumbled across me performing magic. I wouldn't do it now."

"Promise?"

I gave him a kiss. "I promise."

***

We drove home from the hotel in separate cars. I had to stop for fuel, so Jack was already home by the time I got back. He was standing on the pavement, talking to Mr Hosey, who had parked Bessie close to our drive.

"Look what Mr Hosey has done to Bessie." Jack rolled his eyes.

"What do you think, Jill?" Mr Hosey said.

"It's—err—very—err—I don't really understand. You do remember that we said we wouldn't be using Bessie for the wedding, don't you?"

"I know that's what you said, but I thought when you saw how good she looked that you might change your mind. You don't have to worry about the flowers drooping because they're not real. Although, you can hardly tell."

To be fair, he had put in a lot of effort, decorating the engine and carriages. There must have been a thousand (fake) white roses on Bessie, and he'd covered all of the seats in white silk. It looked beautiful, but there was just one minor problem: It was still a stupid train!

"We really do appreciate all the effort you've put into this, Mr Hosey," said Jack—always the diplomat. "But as we mentioned before, the limousines have already been booked. Sorry."

Mr Hosey couldn't have looked any more disappointed. "Oh well. I hope you both have a wonderful day." He climbed into the engine and drove away.

I turned to Jack. "Why do I feel like we've just killed his favourite puppy?"

***

"What time is the nail woman coming," Jack said.

"She's supposed to be here in about thirty minutes, but I wish I'd never agreed to let her do them."

"Why not? You want them to look their best for tomorrow, don't you?"

"Yes, but I'm not sure I trust Deli."

"She's qualified, isn't she?"

"Kind of."

"It'll be fine. She'd hardly have her own shop if she didn't know what she was doing, would she?"

"I suppose not."

"Do you fancy a cup of tea before she comes?"

"Good idea. After she's done them, I won't be able to hold anything for a while."

"I'll put the kettle on. By the way, weren't you

supposed to go to that sports thing today?" He didn't wait for an answer.

As soon as he was out of the door, I magicked myself to CASS. This time, though, I bypassed the west wing, and landed on the playing fields, right next to Reginald Crowe.

"Hi, Reggie."

"Hello there, Jill."

"Are you okay?"

"I'm a bit disgruntled, as it happens."

"Oh? Why's that?"

"You'll never guess what the headmistress had me doing yesterday."

Before I could sympathise with him for having to be the golden-poo collector, someone called my name.

"Jill!" Desdemona Nightowl came hurrying over. "You made it."

"I promised I would."

"The final of the mixed relay is just about to start. Come and watch."

"Who's winning the competition so far?"

"It couldn't be any tighter. There are only three points between the house in first place and the one in last. Whichever house wins the relay will take the trophy."

The headmistress led the way to a small platform where the deputy-head and the heads of house were already seated. On a small table in front of them was the tiniest trophy I'd ever seen.

"Do you like the Gooder Cup?" The headmistress picked it up.

"It's — err — very — err — "

"Small? It is rather, but it was all they had available at such short notice. It worked out rather well because we were able to use the remaining money to refund those who'd had jewellery eaten by Fluff."

I'd envisioned the Gooder Cup as a magnificent trophy. Instead, it was little more than a golden egg cup. Typical.

"Ready, steady, go!"

The final was underway.

The pupils, who were crowded around the track, went wild as each of them cheered on their own team. When the runners passed on the baton for the first time, Wrongacre were in front, followed closely by Nomad, then Longstaff and finally Capstan.

The girl running the second leg for Longstaff was incredibly fast, and by the end of the second lap, she'd put her team in front. Nomad were still second, Wrongacre third, with Capstan still trailing behind.

The third lap resulted in no change to those positions, but the fourth and final lap saw the lead change on more than one occasion. As the runners approached the finish line, Longstaff and Nomad were neck and neck. Moments later, the pupils of Nomad house went wild, as they realised they'd managed to retain the trophy.

A few minutes later, Toyah Harlow, the Nomad house captain, came onto the platform to collect the eggcup — err — trophy.

"Well done, Toyah."

"Thanks, Miss Gooder. We're really proud to be the first house to have our name engraved on the new cup."

Probably the last one, too. There wouldn't be room for any more.

She turned to the crowd and held the tiny trophy aloft.

"Thank you for sparing us your time today, Jill," the headmistress said.

"My pleasure, but I really should get back now."

"Of course. Best wishes for tomorrow."

"Did you hear what I said?" Jack passed me the tea. "Weren't you supposed to go to the sports thing today?"

"I just did."

"When?"

"While you were making the tea. Nomad house won."

"That's just weird. The idea that you could have been over there while I was making a cup of tea is kind of freaky. What's the trophy they named after you like?"

"Magnificent. Probably the biggest one I've ever seen."

I'd just cleared away the empty cups when there was a knock at the door.

"Deli, come in."

"How are you, Jill? I was a bag of nerves the day before we tied the knot."

"I'm okay. Just trying to keep busy."

"Hello, there." Jack made an appearance.

"I can see why you're marrying this one, Jill. I wouldn't chuck him out of bed."

Jack blushed. "I'll leave you ladies to it. I have to — err — do stuff. Upstairs."

"You'd better conserve your energy," Deli shouted after him. "You'll be doing plenty of stuff upstairs tomorrow night."

"Shall we go through to the kitchen?" I said.

"Good idea. You don't want me spilling nail varnish all

over your best carpet, do you? Only kidding!"

"I thought a subtle, natural colour would be best," I said, once I was seated at the kitchen table.

"Don't you go worrying your head about colours. Leave that to the expert. I've done enough brides' nails to know what's what. You trust me, don't you, Jill?"

"Err—yeah, of course."

"Dearie me. You've really neglected these, haven't you?" She studied my nails and shook her head. "They're going to need a lot of prep before I can apply the colour."

"Will it take long?"

"Quite a while, I'm afraid, but don't worry, I've got my secret weapon."

I didn't like the sound of that.

She opened her bag and took out what appeared to be an inflatable neck cushion.

"Slip this around your neck and relax. Doze off if you like. When you wake up, it will all be done."

"I'm not going to fall asleep. I'm wide awake."

"Humour me." She slipped it around my neck.

This was stupid. There was no way I was ever going—

"Jill!"

"What? Where?"

"You were snoring," Jack said.

"Where's Deli?"

"She's gone. She said to tell you she'd collect the cushion another day." He glanced down at my hands. "I didn't realise you were going to have each nail a different colour."

"What?" I screamed.

"I take it you didn't know either."

"I'm going to kill her."

"They don't look all that bad."

I gave him a look.

"Okay, they do look a bit naff."

"I can't get married with my nails looking like this."

"What are you going to do?"

"Jill?" Kathy picked up on the first ring. "Is everything okay?"

"No, it most definitely isn't."

"Don't tell me you and Jack have fallen out. The wedding isn't off, is it?"

"Of course it isn't. Do you have any nail varnish remover at your place?"

"Yes. Why?"

"Good. On your way home, I need you to buy a neutral colour nail varnish."

"Do you want to tell me what's going on?"

"I'll explain later when I get there."

Chapter 19

The big day had arrived.

Nervous? Who me? Of course not. After all the things I'd been through over the last couple of years, why would I be nervous about a little thing like getting married?

"Jill!"

I almost shot out of the chair. "Kathy, why are you sneaking around? You scared me to death."

"I only came in to ask if you wanted another cup of tea."

"I daren't have any more. What if I'm just about to say my vows and I need to pee?"

"You've got three hours before then. If you don't drink, you'll be dehydrated. You don't want to collapse in the middle of the ceremony, do you?"

"Dehydration? Why did you have to mention that? Now I have something else to worry about."

"I thought you said you weren't worried about anything."

"I'm not. Get me a cup of tea, would you? And a glass of water."

I'd stayed the night at Kathy's house. As Peter was going to give me away, it made sense for me to be based there. Jack was back home where his best man, Alby, had stayed overnight.

Kathy had spent much of the previous evening undoing Deli's handiwork. Thankfully, she'd managed to replace the rainbow colours with a neutral colour.

Kathy had been fussing over me since we got up at seven. I'd barely slept all night—I just kept tossing and turning, thinking about all the things that could go wrong.

"When are you putting your dress on, Auntie Jill?" Lizzie was in her PJs.

"Not until it's nearly time for us to go."

"Mummy won't let me put my dress on yet."

"It's probably best not to. You wouldn't want to spill anything on it, would you?"

"I suppose not."

"Where's Mikey?"

"Still in bed." She giggled. "I could hear him snoring — just like a little pig."

"Morning, Jill." Peter appeared behind Lizzie. "She's not annoying you, is she?"

"Daddy!" Lizzie sounded quite indignant. "I'm only *talking* to Auntie Jill."

"It's okay, Peter. She's no trouble at all. How are you? Are you nervous?"

"A little. I've never given anyone away before. Still, it'll be good practice for when this little one gets married." He put his hand on his daughter's shoulder.

"I'm not getting married." Lizzie pulled a face. "Boys are stupid and they all smell." She thought for a moment, and then continued, "Not you, though, Daddy. You're not stupid."

"Thanks."

"You do smell, though. When you come home from work."

"Well, that's me told." He smiled. "Why don't you go and get some breakfast, Petal?"

"Okay. I'm having Sparkle Pops." She dashed out of the room.

"Are you really okay?" Peter asked me.

"I would be if everyone would stop asking if I was okay."

"Sorry."

"No, I'm sorry. I just want to get started. It's the waiting that's the worst part."

"Not long now." He grinned. "Only another two hours and fifty-one minutes."

"The flowers!" I yelled. "Where are the flowers?"

"Were they supposed to be here yet?"

"I'm not sure. Marceau arranged everything. Anyway, where is Marceau?"

"You called?" The man himself popped his head around the door.

"The flowers aren't here yet."

"Have you consulted the wedding day timetable?"

"The what?"

"I gave Jack two copies. Didn't he give you one?"

Just then, a memory from a couple of days earlier, flashed across my mind. Jack had handed me a sheet of paper, and we'd had a brief conversation. I slowly ran it back through my head.

"Jill, this is the timetable."

"The what?"

"The wedding day timetable."

"Why do we need a timetable? Surely, we just turn up, say our vows, and that's it, job done, isn't it?"

"There's a lot more to it than that. Marceau has spent ages drawing this up, so make sure you memorise it, or at least keep it with you."

"Okay."

What had I done with it after that?

Then it came back to me.

Oh no! I'd slipped it into one of the drawers in the

kitchen without even looking at it.

"Jill?" Marceau said. "Did Jack give you a copy?"

"He must have forgotten. You know what he's like."

Marceau harrumphed, and began to fish around in his man-bag. "It's just as well I printed a few additional copies. Here you are. See, the flowers are due to arrive at eleven-thirty-seven."

"Isn't that rather precise?"

"You can never be too precise when it comes to a wedding. I'd better let you get up to speed with the timetable. I have a hundred-and-one calls to make."

To be fair to Marceau, the timetable had every last detail covered. Maybe I should have taken time out to study it before.

***

The flowers arrived at eleven-thirty-seven on the dot. I'm not usually one to gush over flowers, but the bouquets were magnificent. There was only an hour to go until the limousines were due to arrive. Kathy, Lizzie and Mikey would be travelling in the first car; Peter and I would follow in the second.

Kathy and Lizzie looked beautiful in their dresses, and although I do say so myself, I didn't look half bad in mine. The only problem was that I daren't sit down in it, so I was forced to stand and wait until the cars arrived.

Kathy and Peter were keeping the kids occupied in the kitchen, leaving me to contemplate the day ahead, and beyond that, married life with Jack.

When we'd first met, it had been mutual hate at first

sight. Well, that's not strictly true—I'd thought he was hot even then, but he was also a size ten pain in the bum. For reasons that only became clear much later, he'd had a total disdain for private investigators. We'd butted heads numerous times in those early months, but slowly and surely the ice had begun to melt. At some point, our professional relationship had blossomed into something else—we'd fallen in love.

At first, I'd been unsure whether or not we would be able to live together—I'd feared we might end up killing one another. But, against all the odds, it had turned out okay. Anyone who could live with me for a year, and still be sane, must be very special. And Jack was just that—a very special man. Now, we were about to get married. I'd never expected this day to come. I'd assumed that my secret would be an insurmountable obstacle. How could I ever enter into a lifelong commitment with someone while keeping a major part of my life hidden from them? The answer was simple—I couldn't. After Yvonne's tragic death, when Jack had asked me to marry him, I'd known I had to make a decision: Tell him the truth and face the consequences or walk away. Forever.

I was so glad that I'd decided to tell him my secret, and thrilled that he'd been prepared to accept me for who I was.

"Jill." Kathy popped her head around the door. "Madeline Lane is here. Were you expecting her?"

"No."

"She says it's important, but I can send her away if you want me to."

"No, it's okay. Send her in."

Moments later, Mad appeared — a vision in red.

"Wow, Jill, you look amazing!"

"Thanks."

"I'm sorry about dropping in on you like this."

"It's a bit late to change your mind about being a bridesmaid," I teased.

I'd tried to persuade Mad to be a bridesmaid, but she'd have none of it. She'd insisted her mother's wedding was to be her one and only such appearance.

"Someone asked if I'd bring them here to see you this morning."

"Who?"

"Your parents."

Great! That was all I needed. I didn't have time to listen to my mother and father, arguing the toss about the seating arrangements.

"It isn't possible to change the seating plan now. I've already explained they'll have to sit at the back."

Mad shook her head. "I don't mean your birth parents."

"Sorry?"

"Your adoptive parents would like to see you."

I felt as though someone had pulled the floor from under my feet, and I slumped back onto the sofa.

"Should you be sitting down in your dress?" Mad said. "Jill, are you okay?"

"Did you just say my *adoptive* parents?"

"Yeah. They turned up first thing this morning and asked if I thought you'd mind if they came to see you."

At that, I burst into tears.

"I'm sorry if I did the wrong thing by bringing them here, Jill."

"No." I snuffled. "You didn't. I just—err—I wasn't expecting—where are they?"

"Outside. I said I'd come and talk to you first."

"Would you go and get them, please?"

"Sure." She disappeared out of the room.

Somehow, I struggled back to my feet. My heart was racing, and it felt as though it might burst out of my chest.

Moments later, Mad reappeared. Standing next to her were my parents; the two people who had raised me from a baby.

"Mum. Dad," I said through my tears.

"I hope you don't mind us coming here today." Hearing my mother's voice again after so many years was wonderful.

"We weren't sure if we should come or not." Dad sounded exactly the same as the last time I'd spoken to him.

"I'll leave you to it." Mad slipped quietly out of the room.

"We aren't very good at this 'ghost thing'." Mum smiled that wonderful smile of hers. "It's the first time we've ever done it."

"I had no idea you were in Ghost Town. I'd have come to see you ages ago."

"We're not," Dad said. "It never really appealed to us to stop off there. We had to apply for special permission to come here today. We can only stay for a few minutes, and then we have to go back."

"Surely, you'll stay for the wedding?"

"We'd love to, but we simply can't," Mum said. "That's why we wanted to catch you before the ceremony, so we could have some time with you alone."

"Why don't you move to Ghost Town? I could see you all the time then."

"I'm sorry, Jill. Ghost Town simply isn't for us."

"Are you happy where you are?"

"Very. We miss you of course. Kathy too."

"She's just next door. I could go and get her."

"It wouldn't do any good. She wouldn't be able to see us. The only reason you can is because you're a—" She hesitated. "Is it okay to call you a witch?"

"Of course it is. Did you always know?"

"That you were a witch?" She laughed. "Of course not. How could we?"

"How do you feel about it?" Dad asked.

"It was pretty weird at first, but I've kind of got used to it now."

"What about your birth parents?" Mum said. "How do you get on with them?"

"Okay. They're good people, but you two will always be my mum and dad."

Mum's eyes filled with tears.

Dad looked close to tears too, but he managed to say, "How's the business going?"

"Okay. I'll never be as good a P.I. as you, but I get by okay."

"I'm sure you're doing brilliantly."

"What's this young man of yours like?" Mum asked. "I hear his name is Jack."

"He's great. He's probably the only person, apart from you two, who actually gets me."

"Does he know—err—about the witch thing?"

"We don't have any secrets."

"That's as it should be. Come on, then, turn around, and

let me have a good look at your dress."

I did as she asked. "Kathy helped me to choose it. She has her own bridal shop now."

"Does she? How fantastic. I managed to get a quick glance at her kids when Madeline brought us in just now. They're so like Kathy."

Suddenly, Mum started to wheeze.

"Are you okay?"

"This ghost thing really takes it out of you. I think we'll have to be getting back."

"Already? Can't you stay for just a little longer?"

"I'm sorry, Jill." Her image was already starting to fade.

"Will I see you again?"

"I'm not sure. Maybe someday. We love you."

"Sorry, Jill." Dad took her hand. "We have to—"

And just like that, they were gone.

Moments later, Kathy came into the room. "Are you okay, Jill?"

"Yeah, I'm fine."

"Are you sure? You look like you've just seen a ghost."

"I'm okay, honestly. Just fed up of waiting."

"Not long now. What did Madeline want?"

"Nothing, really. Just to wish me all the best."

"Silly girl. She didn't need to disturb you just for that."

"It's okay. I'm really glad she did."

***

The limousines were due at any moment. Peter and the kids were outside, keeping a lookout for them. Marceau had gone on ahead in his own car.

Kathy and I were in the lounge.

"Mum and Dad would have been so proud of you today," Kathy said, totally out of the blue. "I wish they could have been here." She began to well up.

"They are here. In spirit, anyway."

"You're right." She wiped away a tear. "I'm sure they're looking down on us right now."

"The cars are here!" Peter shouted. "The first one, anyway."

Moments later, a white limousine pulled up outside the house.

"This is us." Kathy gave me a kiss. "We'll see you there."

Peter and I watched as Kathy and the kids climbed into the car and drove away.

"Nervous yet?" he asked.

"Terrified."

"You'll be okay once you get there. It's the waiting that's the worst part."

"Here it comes." I pointed to the limousine which had just turned onto our street.

"You're supposed to be at the hotel by two, aren't you?" the driver asked once we were seated in the back.

"A bit before then," Peter said. "The ceremony starts at two."

"We may have a problem, then."

Those were not the words I wanted to hear at that precise moment in time.

"What do you mean?" I barked.

"All the roads around Washbridge Park are gridlocked with traffic headed to the music festival."

"Will we make it?"

"I'm not sure. Hopefully."

"Let's get going then."

The first part of the journey, from Smallwash to Washbridge, went smoothly enough, but as soon as we reached the outskirts of the city, the traffic ground to a halt.

"Why didn't Marceau think about this?" I said to no one in particular.

"I'm sorry, lady, but I can't see us making it there on time," the driver said. "You might be better getting out and walking."

"From here? It must be two miles. We'll never make it, and besides, I can barely walk in these heels."

"I'll call Kathy." Peter grabbed his phone. "Kathy, we're stuck in traffic. You too? Where are you?"

Someone knocked on the side-window. It was Mr Hosey, reaching out from the cab of Bessie. He motioned for me to wind down the window.

"I thought you might have problems today," he said. "I heard about the congestion on Washbridge Radio."

"Who's that?" Peter asked.

"It's one of our neighbours."

"Come on." Mr Hosey beckoned to us. "Jump on board."

"I can't turn up to my wedding on that thing."

"It's the only way you'll get there on time. Bessie can drive along the pavement."

"He's right," Peter said. "What choice do we have? And besides, it does look really good with all those flowers. They must have cost him a small fortune."

So off we set. I did my best to ignore all the strange looks we got as we made our way through the streets.

"Look, Kathy and the kids are over there!" Peter shouted.

"Mr Hosey. Can you pick those people up?"

"No problem." He pulled up alongside Kathy whose face by now was a picture.

"Don't ask." I pre-empted her questions.

"This is great, Auntie Jill," Lizzie said.

"Totally cool." Mikey agreed.

Chapter 20

Despite the bumpy ride, and the strange looks that we'd attracted along the way, Bessie managed to deliver us to the hotel with ten minutes to spare. Mad, who was standing outside the main doors, signalled that she wanted a word.

"There you go," Mr Hosey said. "All safe and sound."

"Thanks." I was trying my best to get out of the small carriage without snagging my dress.

"You can call this my wedding present to you both."

"Thanks again."

He tooted his whistle, and away he steamed.

"You lot go inside," I said to Kathy, Peter and the kids. "I'll be in in a couple of minutes."

"Don't you dare run away." Kathy looked genuinely concerned.

"I'm not going anywhere. I just need a quick word with Mad."

"If you'd told me you were going to travel here by model train, I'd have come with you." Mad grinned.

"It wasn't planned, I can assure you. The roads are all gridlocked. Has everyone else made it?"

"I think so because there's a full house inside. I hope you didn't mind my bringing your adoptive parents over earlier? I didn't know what to do for the best."

"I'm really pleased you did. I didn't think I'd ever see them again."

Kathy appeared in the doorway. "Come on. It's five-to."

"Okay. I'm coming."

"Jill, wait." Mad caught me by the arm. "There's

someone who has been waiting for you." She gestured to the side of the hotel.

"Who is it? I really should go inside."

"It'll only take a minute. Come and see."

"Winky?"

"I'll leave you to it." Mad made her exit.

"I thought you were never going to get here." He looked super smart in his tux. "Did you go to the wrong hotel too?"

"I—err—"

"I know you've been stressed about the wedding, but how did you manage to mix up the names of the hotels? When I realised your mistake, I had to hightail it over here from the Washbridge Hotel. You're lucky I made it at all. We'd better get inside."

"Winky, I—err—I don't know how to say—"

"Come on. I'm really looking forward to this."

Oh bum!

I'd painted myself into a corner this time. If I told him now that he couldn't be my pagecat, he'd be totally devastated, but if I allowed everyone to see him, they'd think I'd lost my mind.

That's when it came to me: a way to get out of this awful mess.

I quickly cast the 'hide' spell.

"Okay. Follow me, but once we're inside, you mustn't speak. At all."

"I won't. I promise."

"You have to walk behind the two bridesmaids."

"No problem."

"And be careful where you step. You mustn't bump

into anyone."

"Okay, okay. Let's go."

I hurried inside to find Kathy, Peter and Lizzie waiting outside the room where the ceremony was to take place.

"I thought you were never coming." Kathy looked more than a little flustered.

"I'm here now. Let's do this."

Peter took my arm, and Kathy and Lizzie fell in behind us. Moments later, when the music started, we walked through the door.

The next twenty minutes are a bit of a blur. I remember Jack looking back at me as I walked down the aisle; the smile on his face blew away all of my nerves. We made our vows and moments later, kissed for the first time as man and wife.

"We did it," Jack said, as we walked through the French doors out onto the large patio.

Before I could reply, we were showered with confetti.

"How does it feel to be Mrs Maxwell?" Jack brushed a piece of confetti from his mouth.

"It feels great."

"I hear you had a few problems getting here."

"We did, but Mr Hosey came to our rescue."

"You came here on Bessie?" He laughed.

"I just hope no one took any photos."

"It'll be something to tell our kids."

"You'll never guess who came to see me this morning."

"It wasn't more clowns, was it?"

"No, thank goodness. It was my mum and dad."

"They were in church, weren't they?"

"I mean my adoptive parents. I haven't seen them

since—well, since they died."

"That must have been a shock."

"It was, but the best one ever."

"I was kind of hoping that my mum might—" His words trailed away.

"She will, Jack. One day. I'm sure she will. Give her time."

The next thirty minutes or so were taken up posing for a million and one photographs. Marceau had hired the photographer—a man by the name of Brian Lyon. He was a fussy little so and so, who took an eternity on every shot.

"Why is he taking so many?" I said under my breath, as Jack and I posed for the millionth photo.

"When we're old and grey, and we look at our wedding album, you'll be pleased that he did."

"At this rate, it'll be our silver wedding anniversary before he's finished."

While Brian (who should have been named Sloth) Lyon took photos of the guests, I managed to escape to the other side of the lawn where Kathy and Peter were having a breather.

"I think it all went okay in there," I said.

"Jack looks amazing," Kathy glanced over at him.

"What about me?"

"You look okay too." She gave me a hug. "I'm only kidding. You look fantastic, sis. Mind you, I'd have a few words with the hotel manager if I were you."

"What about?"

"Didn't you smell it?"

"Smell what?"

"When we were walking down the aisle, I got the definite whiff of cat."

"Yeah." Peter nodded. "So did I."

"I reckon they must have left a cat in that room overnight," Kathy said. "You should complain."

"Err—excuse me for a moment, would you?"

I'd completely forgotten about Winky. Where could he be?

I eventually found him leaning against a tree, looking very pleased with himself.

"So? What do you think?" he said.

"About what?"

"Did I make a good pagecat or what?"

"You—err—"

"I know what you're thinking. You're thinking, that cat is a natural. And you'd be correct. I blended in so well that no one seemed to think it was odd that I was part of the ceremony. Did you notice that?"

"I did notice that." He obviously had no idea that no one could see him. "I don't imagine you'll want to stay for the reception? It'll be terribly boring."

"Are you joking? All that food and drink? That's the best part. Am I on the top table?"

"Err—no, that's just for family. I'm afraid you're at the back of the room."

"Never mind. As long as there's plenty of salmon, I'll be happy."

"Jill!" Jack came hurrying over. "The photographer needs us again."

"Okay, I'm coming."

"Who were you talking to over there?"

"Just my invisible cat."

"I never know whether you're joking or not these days."

***

Eventually, the photographer announced he'd finished, so we were able to go inside to the Crimson Room where the meal was to be served. Jack took my hand and led me to the top table where Kathy, Peter, Lizzie, Mikey, Grandma and Aunt Lucy were already seated. Also there, was Jack's father, Roy.

Mrs V, who was on one of the front tables with Armi, Jules and Dexter, gave me a little wave. On the table next to them were the twins, Alan, William and Daze. Alan's mother had volunteered to babysit the two Lils. At the table at the far side of the room were my birth mother and father, and their partners, Alberto and Blodwyn. Of course, to the majority of people, that particular table appeared to be empty.

"Where's the food?" I whispered to Jack. "I'm starving."

"It's the speeches first."

"I thought they came afterwards."

"Marceau reckons it's best to get them out of the way first, so that everyone can relax and enjoy their meal."

At that moment, Peter struck his glass with a spoon. "Ladies and gentlemen. It was my great honour today to give away my sister-in-law, Jill. I'd like to say a few words which I hope her father, Ken, would have approved of."

For the next few minutes, Peter spoke eloquently and from the heart. When he'd finished, I leaned over and said, "Thanks. Dad would definitely have approved."

Jack was next up.

"On behalf of my wife and myself." The corny opening line drew polite applause. "First, I'd like to thank Peter for standing in for Jill's father today. I'd also like to thank all of you for coming here to celebrate our marriage. And of course, I mustn't forget Alby, my best man, who made sure I got through the stag night unscathed. Relatively speaking." He took a sip of water, and then continued, "Today, I feel like the luckiest man in the whole world. Some of you may already know that I lost my mother just over a year ago. My parents were a shining example of what a marriage could be. I never thought I'd find someone who could make me as happy as my mother made my father, but then I met Jill. Even though we didn't immediately see eye to eye, I very quickly realised there was something very special about her." He turned to me. "I just didn't know *how* special. Jill, I want to thank you for agreeing to be my wife. I look forward to spending the rest of our lives together." With that he held up his glass. "Please join me in a toast to the bridesmaids, Kathy and Lizzie, who I'm sure you'll agree look absolutely amazing. The bridesmaids."

Alby was as nervous as a kitten, and his speech wasn't the best, but he managed to struggle through it.

At long last, it was time for us to eat. I was ravenous.

"I'm sorry to bother you." One of the waiters appeared at my side. "A woman asked me to hand this to you. She said it was urgent." He passed me a small white envelope, which I assumed was another card. "She said to mention her name was Chivers."

"Where is she?" I looked around the room.

"She left as soon as she'd handed it to me."

"Okay, thanks."

I ripped open the envelope, and read the note inside:

Alicia sends her apologies that she couldn't be at your wedding, but she doesn't have long to live. Just a few minutes, actually. Just long enough for the scarlet to spill her blood.
Best wishes,
Ma.

I'd suspected all along that Ma Chivers had had something to do with Alicia's disappearance. Not only did the note confirm that, but it also made it clear that her life was in imminent danger. Scarlet? If that meant what I thought it did, Alicia was in big trouble.

"Jack," I whispered. "I have to nip out."

"What? Why? They're just about to serve the meal."

"I'm sorry. It's a matter of life and death."

"Come with me." He led the way out into the garden where we could speak without being overheard. "What's going on?"

"A friend — err — well, not exactly a friend, but someone I know is in danger. If I don't go to Candlefield now, she'll be killed for sure."

"Killed how?"

I hesitated.

"Jill? Tell me."

"If my hunch is correct, she's just about to become a meal for a scarlet horned dragon."

"Very funny." He smiled, but then realised I wasn't joking. "You're being serious, aren't you?"

"I'm afraid so."

"It sounds dangerous."

"It isn't. Well, not really. I've fought one before."

"What shall I tell everyone?"

"You won't need to tell them anything. Have you forgotten that time stands still here while I'm in Candlefield?"

"I'll never get used to that." He gave me a kiss. "Promise you'll be careful."

"Of course I will." I did a quick check to make sure there was no one else around, and then magicked myself to the Range in Candlefield.

The place was deserted except for a scarlet horned dragon, which was making its way towards the far wall, where a woman was chained to a metal pole. Even from that distance, I could see the terror on Alicia's face as the dragon advanced towards her.

I used the 'faster' spell to speed across the ground, and then placed myself between the dragon and its would-be meal.

"Jill?" Alicia's voice was very weak.

"It's going to be okay."

The dragon seemed undeterred by my arrival; if anything, it seemed buoyed by the prospect of double helpings. After a moment's hesitation, it charged straight at me. It didn't get far though. The first lightning bolt slowed it down — the second one sent it scurrying away.

Once I was sure it wasn't coming back for another go, I set about releasing Alicia from her shackles.

"I thought I was a goner." She was breathing heavily. "Ma blocked my magic, so I couldn't do anything."

"Don't worry. I'll unblock it before I go back."

Only then, did she seem to register my attire. "What are you wearing, Jill? It looks like a wedding dress."

"I've just got married to Jack. We were about to sit down to the wedding meal when I got a note from Ma Chivers saying you were about to meet a grisly end."

"I'll never be able to thank you enough." She gave me a hug.

"Enough of that. I have to get back. Will you be okay now?"

"Yeah, I'm fine, thanks. It's great to be free again."

I unblocked her magic, and then magicked myself back. I'd no sooner arrived in the hotel garden than Kathy appeared.

"Are you alright? They're serving the starters."

"Honestly, I'm fine."

"Are you sure? I thought you'd gone outside because you were feeling off it."

"Really, I'm fine. Let's get back inside."

"What happened to your dress?"

I glanced down to see that the bottom of it was covered in mud from the Range.

"I—err—it's quite muddy over there." I pointed to nowhere in particular. "It'll brush off. Come on, let's get inside. I'm starving."

"Are you okay?" Jack said when I took my seat next to him.

"Yeah. I'm fine."

"And your friend?"

"She's okay."

"What about the dragon?"

"He's not feeling so good. His legs will be sore for a few days. Now, where's that soup?"

The caterers had done us proud. All three courses were delicious, and judging by the empty plates on most of the tables, everyone else thought so too.

"Jill," someone whispered in my ear.

"Mum?"

"Can I have a word, please?"

"Just a second." I turned to Jack. "Sorry. My mother wants a word with me."

He looked around. "Where is she?"

"Right behind me."

"Hi," he said in her general direction. "I'm sorry you couldn't sit up here with us."

"Who are you talking to?" Kathy chimed in.

While Jack tried to explain his strange behaviour to Kathy, I followed my mother out into the corridor.

"Is something wrong?"

"I don't like to complain, Jill, but when you said we'd have to sit at the back, I didn't realise we wouldn't actually get any food."

Oh bum! When I'd agreed that my parents would take the 'empty' table at the back of the room, it hadn't occurred to me that they wouldn't be fed.

"I'm really sorry."

"It's okay. We don't want to make a big fuss. If you could just see your way clear to grabbing a few nibbles for us, that would help."

"Of course. I'll go and see what I can get now."

"Thanks, Jill. I'd have done it myself, but I thought it might cause a few raised eyebrows if the nibbles suddenly started to float away. We'll be in that small room across the corridor. No one will see us eating in there."

"Okay. I'll be as quick as I can."

"Oh, and Jill, while you're at it. See if you can find any salmon. That invisible cat of yours has been driving us insane."

"I'm very angry with you," Winky said when I delivered the food to the side room.

"Why? I've just brought some salmon for you."

"You made me invisible."

"You know?"

"Yes, I know. Why would you do something like that?"

"I'm sorry, but it would have been too difficult to explain why I had a pagecat."

"All the effort I put into my outfit, and posing for photographs. Totally wasted."

"It wasn't wasted. You were an important part of the ceremony."

"When no one could see me?"

"I could see you, and that's all that matters. You looked great. I was proud to have you as my pagecat."

"Really? Are you just saying that?"

"No. I mean it. It wouldn't have been the same without you."

"I did look good, didn't I?"

"Absolutely. And I'm really sorry I had to make you invisible."

"Sorry enough to make it up to me?"

"Err—what did you have in mind?" As if I didn't already know.

"Salmon every day for a month when you get back

from honeymoon."

"Okay."

"Red not pink, obviously."

"Obviously."

On my way back to join Jack, the twins intercepted me.

"You look really beautiful today, Jill." Amber gave me a hug.

"Thanks."

"Yeah, you and Jack make a great couple," Pearl said.

"Thanks, girls. That means a lot."

"Where are you going on honeymoon?"

"If I told you that, I'd have to kill you both."

Just then, the DJ put on a slow number.

"I'd better get back to William," Amber gave me a quick peck on the cheek. "They're playing our song."

"That's mine and Alan's song!" Pearl said, but Amber was already on her way back across the dancefloor.

"Are you and Alan having a good time?" I said.

"Great, thanks, but we miss Lily."

"*Lily*? Don't you mean Lil?"

"Not any longer. Alan and I decided it's silly for both girls to be called by the same name, so from now on our little girl will be known as Lily. That should avoid any confusion."

I wouldn't bank on it. "That sounds like a great idea. I assume you haven't mentioned this to Amber yet?"

"We haven't told anyone yet. We only decided last

night."

"You should definitely tell Amber."

"I will. Anyway, have a lovely honeymoon wherever it is you're going."

"Thanks."

So long, Lil and Lil. Hello, Lily and Lily.

Snigger.

***

The rest of the day went without a hitch. After I'd changed out of my wedding dress, Jack and I danced the night away, and as far as I could tell, everyone had a great time.

"It's time we called it a day," Jack said when it had just turned eleven-thirty. "We have an early flight in the morning."

"I don't want this day to end."

"Who said it has ended?" He led the way upstairs to the honeymoon suite where we —

Never you mind what we got up to. Let's just say, it was magical.

ALSO BY ADELE ABBOTT

The Witch P.I. Mysteries
(A Candlefield/Washbridge Series)

Witch Is When... (Books #1 to #12)
Witch Is When It All Began
Witch Is When Life Got Complicated
Witch Is When Everything Went Crazy
Witch Is When Things Fell Apart
Witch Is When The Bubble Burst
Witch Is When The Penny Dropped
Witch Is When The Floodgates Opened
Witch Is When The Hammer Fell
Witch Is When My Heart Broke
Witch Is When I Said Goodbye
Witch Is When Stuff Got Serious
Witch Is When All Was Revealed

Witch Is Why... (Books #13 to #24)
Witch Is Why Time Stood Still
Witch is Why The Laughter Stopped
Witch is Why Another Door Opened
Witch is Why Two Became One
Witch is Why The Moon Disappeared
Witch is Why The Wolf Howled
Witch is Why The Music Stopped
Witch is Why A Pin Dropped
Witch is Why The Owl Returned
Witch is Why The Search Began
Witch is Why Promises Were Broken
Witch is Why It Was Over

Witch Is How... (Books #25 to #36)
Witch is How Things Had Changed
Witch is How Berries Tasted Good
Witch is How The Mirror Lied
Witch is How The Tables Turned
Witch is How The Drought Ended
Witch is How The Dice Fell
Witch is How The Biscuits Disappeared
Witch is How Dreams Became Reality
Witch is How Bells Were Saved
Witch is How To Fool Cats
Witch is How To Lose Big
Witch is How Life Changed Forever

Susan Hall Investigates
(A Candlefield/Washbridge Series)
Whoops! Our New Flatmate Is A Human.
Whoops! All The Money Went Missing.
Whoops! Someone Is On Our Case.

Web site: AdeleAbbott.com
Facebook: facebook.com/AdeleAbbottAuthor
Instagram: #adele_abbott_author